AVENGER FROM HELL

AVENGER FROM HELL

WILL BLACK

A Black Horse Western

ROBERT HALE · LONDON

© Will Black 1997
First published in Great Britain 1997

ISBN 0 7090 5803 9

Robert Hale Limited
Clerkenwell House
Clerkenwell Green
London EC1R 0HT

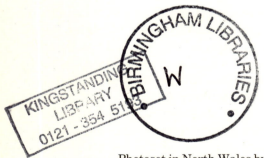

Photoset in North Wales by
Derek Doyle & Associates, Mold, Clwyd.
Printed and bound in Great Britain by
WBC Ltd, Bridgend, Mid-Glamorgan.

To Ray Wright
– at least I got you reading again!

ONE

The Wells Fargo stagecoach ground to a halt in a cloud of dust. Sweat from both horses and driver dripped silently into the parched ground, disappearing without a trace as the sun blazed down mercilessly.

Noon in Tumbleweed during the summer months was a place no sane person wanted to be.

Hal Warton was no sane man. In his late thirties, he'd been released from prison three days ago. Ten bucks in his pocket, he knew exactly where he was headed. Tall, lean and mean, a mane of black hair spilling out either side of his black Stetson, Hal stepped down from the stagecoach and eased his aching muscles.

The driver threw down his brown leather bag and that, too, sent up a cloud of dust that clogged the air. Hal glared at the man, but didn't say anything. He took out a small cigar, flicked a match on his thumbnail and lit it. Inhaling deeply, he looked round the almost deserted main street of Tumbleweed.

Sun-bleached clapboard buildings stared back

at him. Everything was coated in a fine layer of yellow sand making the town look what it was – uncared for.

From behind closed windows Hal caught sight of faces peering out at the stagecoach and, more important, its occupants. Hal Warton was the only passenger. The driver, still unloading mail, catalogue goods and seed bags, kept his eye on the tall stranger who'd not uttered a word to him all day.

Ben Chisolm had been driving for Wells Fargo for nearly a year, the trip between Tumbleweed and Harks Crossing had become as familiar to him as the back of his hand, but this was the first time a single passenger had not joined him up top for the trip where it was usually cooler and which enabled to Ben to partake of his favourite hobby – talking.

Without turning, Hal Warton walked towards the Silver Dollar saloon and pushed through the batwing doors. The saloon was deserted – even the barkeep was missing. Hal walked up to the counter and banged his fist down, hard.

A voice came from behind the counter. Slim Downes, fifty if he was day and wrinkled more like a seventy-year-old, struggled up to his feet.

'Gol-damnit!' he muttered through broken, blackened teeth. 'Cain't a man grab a nap without bein' woked up?'

'Beer,' Hal Warton ordered.

Slim was about to continue complaining when he caught sight of the steely glint in the stranger's eyes and thought better of it. He drew a beer and slid it down the counter.

Hal retrieved the glass and downed it without drawing breath.

'Another!' he bellowed, 'an' a chaser.'

Slim pulled the beer and poured the whiskey. 'Leave the bottle,' Hal said.

Slim did as he was told.

Although the beer was warm and virtually tasteless, it took the trail dust from Hal's mouth. The whiskey however, tasted good – real good.

Hal grabbed the bottle and tumbler and sat at a table in the corner of the deserted saloon. He wouldn't move until the bottle was empty.

Hal had only been in the saloon for fifteen minutes when the small, fat man wearing a tin star entered. He stood and looked at Hal, tipped his hat and headed for the counter.

'Beer, Slim,' the sheriff said as he took his hat off and mopped his brow.

Slim drew the beer and made himself look busy.

'Howdy, stranger,' Tom Devlin said to Hal. 'Stayin' round town long?'

'Might be, then again, might not,' Hal replied sipping another whiskey.

'Got ourselves a peaceful town here, mister,' Devlin said.

'So?' Hal drained his glass.

'So, we aim to keep it that way,' Devlin replied.

'Talk to all strangers thataway, Sheriff?'

'Some, some not.'

Hal refilled his tumbler and downed it. He

never took his eyes off the fat man. Devlin began to feel uncomfortable. This was a small backwater town, nothing ever happened here, that's why he was sheriff, but this man looked like trouble to Devlin and the sweat that was running down his face wasn't just caused by the heat of the day.

He took a neckerchief from his back pocket and nervously wiped his forehead and the inside brim of his battered, dust-stained Stetson. Tom Devlin aimed to stay alive as well as stay as sheriff of Tumbleweed and the only way he knew how to do that was to compromise. Devlin was good at compromise. Some folk called it being chicken, but Tom Devlin was still alive.

'Didn't mean anythin' by it, mister,' he said at last. 'But, bein' sheriff an' all, I gotta do my duty.'

'Consider it done, Sheriff' Hal Warton said. 'Now, 'less there's anything else, I aim to do me a mess o' drinkin' afore I turn in.'

'Well, I'd be proud to stand you one,' Devlin said, a sickly grin spreading over his sweat filled face.

'I drink alone,' Warton said.

For a few moments, Tom Devlin stood there looking like a prize idiot, embarrassment was unknown to him; to be embarrassed, you had to have some sensibility. Devlin had none.

The four of five men that had entered the saloon were staring at their sheriff with a look of total disgust, but Devlin ignored them and said,

'Well, maybe next time.'

Hal Warton didn't even look towards the man.

He continued drinking as Devlin left the saloon, looking neither left nor right.

During the course of the evening, the saloon began to fill. Townsfolk in for a drink after a day's work, cowboys in from the local ranches. All male, not a woman in sight.

Hal Warton had finished his bottle of rot-gut and had consumed seven glasses of beer. He was ready for female company.

'Barkeep,' he called out to Slim. 'Where's a man git a woman in this hell hole?'

Slim Downes immediately left the cowpoke he was serving and walked down the far end of the bar, opposite to where Warton was sitting.

'There's a house, down Main a ways,' Slim said. 'Might not be anyone there though.'

'What sorta whorehouse is that?' Warton demanded.

'Well, it ain't a *real* whorehouse,' Slim added. 'But Miss Lucy sure can be accommodating at times.'

Hal grinned. He'd met accommodating women before. Not for a long time, admittedly. Prison sure made a man feel sassy.

Downing his last beer, Warton left the saloon on legs that felt decidedly unsteady and not unnoticed by the rest of the clientele. Once outside the fresh air hit him like a sledgehammer and he rested, leaning on a hitching pole that was hanging on in the dirt for grim life. Hal even thought at the time that if anyone was stupid enough to hitch their horse to this pole, both horse and pole would be long gone by sun up.

Steadying himself, he began to lurch down Main, meandering in the general direction given by Slim.

Dusk had fallen like a heavy blanket across the sky. To the west, a deep-red glow illuminated the flat horizon tinged with a faint yellow halo, then nothing, starless blackness for as far as the eye could see. Not that Hal Warton took the time to look. He was too busy making sure his feet hit the ground in some semblance of forward motion.

The journey – which was no more than a hundred yards – wound its way out to at least two hundred as Hal fought to maintain a sense of soberness he didn't feel.

Ahead, and slightly to his left was the house Slim had described. Red drapes adorned the windows all but blocking out the light that shone from within.

Hal grinned and licked his lips lasciviously. He wanted a woman – any woman – and this Miss Lucy was as good as any, even though he'd never seen her. Straightening himself up, he wiped his face with a bandanna, hitched his Levis up a notch, belched and climbed the three steps to the porch which proved a mite harder than he imagined.

He almost fell, but held on to a rough, white painted balustrade that ran up one side of the short flight. He took three or four deep breaths, trying to sober himself up as best he could. Then knocked on the door.

Hal stood there, swaying slightly, as if he were upright in a strong wind, waiting for his knock to be answered.

From behind the frosted glass of the front door a light appeared, moving from side to side as it was carried down the hallway. The light paused, hovering like a giant glow-worm.

'Who's there?' a voice asked.

'Me, ma'am,' Hal answered, trying to keep the slur from his voice that he knew was there.

'Well, that's a damn help,' the voice replied.

The door opened – wide – revealing a woman who must have been a good looker once upon a time.

Lucy Montgomery was thirty-eight, stood five-feet-three in her boots and was at least that in girth. She had big, brown eyes that showed she'd seen plenty of good times. Bright, they glinted in the light of the oil-lamp she was holding. Her long brown hair fell to her shoulders and Hal couldn't take his eyes off her ruby-red-painted, full lips that smiled at him revealing perfect white teeth.

'Well, now. What we got here,' she said.

Hal stood and stared at her mouth, then his eyes fell to her bosom. He'd not seen a chest like that in many a year.

'Evenin', ma'am,' Warton said, trying to tip his hat as he spoke. 'Slim, over to the saloon said you was, well, you know. So I thought I'd mosey on over over and introduce myself. Warton's the name, Hal Warton.'

'Slim said I was what, exactly, Mr Warton?'

For the first time in his life, Hal Warton reddened. He also became tongue-tied, and while his mouth wanted to say something – anything – his mind didn't come up with the words he needed to say. Instead, his open mouth said nothing.

'Come in, Mr Warton,' Lucy smiled at him. She knew she'd won, there was no need to labour the point.

Lucy Montgomery stood to one side of the door. 'Come in, mister,' she said, a grin lighting up her face.

*   *   *

Frankie Warren, deputy sheriff, began his morning rounds. Young, twenty-two in a few weeks, he was full of his own importance.

In truth, Tumbleweed didn't need a deputy, Tom Devlin did. Without a deputy, Devlin knew he'd have to do all the work himself, and that wasn't in his character.

Badge shining brightly in the morning sun, Frankie strutted down Main Street. Shirt pressed, clean jeans and waistcoat, he knew he looked good. Standing just a tad over six feet, broad-shouldered, fair-haired and blue-eyed, nobody loved Frankie Warren more than Frankie Warren.

As was his custom, he checked doors and windows of the saloon, the livery stable, the store, the hotel, then walked down the back alleys, making sure there'd been no break-ins or bums sleeping off the drink of the night before.

Frankie liked it when he found a sleeping drunk in a back alley. He liked to cock his gun right in their ear and yell loudly to wake them up so he could see the look of fear on their faces. Kids, Frankie was fond of ordering them around, too. He wasn't too keen on dealing with men his own size.

The town was quiet, it was rarely anything else these days. The days of the wagon trains and trail herds passing through had long gone. There were better routes and bigger towns to the West now for the settlers to lay over and where the people went, the cattle followed.

Frankie thought back to the good old days, the gunfights, the saloon brawls. He'd only been a kid then, but he'd already decided to be a lawman. It was the glamour he was after, the hero-worship of the townsfolk. But times had changed, all he was now was a glorified watchman.

He drew his Colt and twirled it a few times, then slammed it back in his holster. Drew again, cocked it, released the hammer, and re-holstered again. He'd like to do it for real – as long as he knew he'd win of course.

Hal Warton stood and watched the young deputy go through his practice draws. A steely grin that didn't reach his eyes spread over his mouth as, with clenched teeth holding the remains of a cigar he began to clap his hands slowly.

Frankie Warren turned round so quickly he

almost lost his balance.

'Playin' on your own, kid?' Hal said.

'I ain't playin', mister,' Frankie said.

'Looked that way to me.'

'Jus' practisin', is all,' Frankie said. He looked at the tall stranger and didn't like what he saw. The man looked as mean as a rattler and Frankie noticed his top-coat was already pegged back behind his sideiron.

'Maybe you should try it for real,' Hal said, spreading his legs slightly and digging his heels into the sand.

'I ain't got no argument with you, mister,' Frankie said.

'Maybe not,' Hal replied, 'but I still reckon you should try it for real.'

Frankie had already lifted his hand well away from his gun, he didn't want any misunderstanding. 'I said I ain't got no argument with you, mister. Let's jus' leave it at that.'

'Reckon you're yeller, kid,' Hal said. 'I can see that streak o' yeller run plumb down the centre o' your back.'

Hal Warton was enjoying himself. Although this kid wasn't one of the men he'd come here to get even with, he'd taken an instant dislike to the man.

'Ain't no call for that, mister,' Frankie said.

'You tellin' me I'm wrong, boy?' Hal said.

'No.'

'You sayin' I cain't see no yeller streak?'

'Now look, mister ...'

'I reckon you're callin' me a liar, boy,' Hal said and his right hand rested on the butt of his gun.

From behind him, Hal heard footsteps. Moving a foot, he positioned himself so that by looking straight ahead, he could see both men out of the corner of his eye.

Warton recognized Devlin straight away, there couldn't be that many people that fat in Tumbleweed.

'You okay, Frankie?' Devlin asked.

The look of relief of Frankie Warren's face was all too apparent.

'Sure, sure, Sheriff,' he said, sweat running freely down his back.

'Boy's jus' called me a liar, Sheriff,' Hal said, still looking directly at neither man.

Devlin, too, began to sweat. He'd not liked the look of this *hombre* from the moment he'd first set eyes on him. He was bad. Devlin knew that, and the last thing he wanted was a gunfight.

'I'm sure the boy didn't mean no harm,' Devlin stammered out. 'Let's jus' all relax and go about our business, eh?'

'Cain't do that, Sheriff,' Warton said. 'No man calls me a liar.'

'I ain't called you no liar, mister,' Warren said, the tremble in his voice coming through loud and clear.

'Ain't the way I figured it, boy,' Hal said.

'Then I 'pologize,' Warren said.

'Ain't good enough. I demand satisfaction, boy. My honour's at stake here, how would it look if this got round town?' Hal Warton stood his ground.

'Now look here, mister,' Devlin began and as Hal shifted his eyesight, Frankie Warren made the biggest – and last – mistake of his young life.

Thinking he'd have the drop on the stranger, Frankie went for his gun in the same way he'd done it a thousand times before, standing in front of a mirror, or kids, or a window where he could see his own reflection. Never in front of another man, and never in front of another man who had a gun.

Frankie drew; to Devlin, he drew as quick as a lightning strike, but Hal Warton was quicker. Warton was quicker, because he knew the boy would draw, that's why he'd looked away.

Frankie Warren's gun went off, but in his nervous hand the bullet meant for Hal's back missed by a mile. The .45 from Hal's gun punched a hole in Frankie Warren's chest then threw him backwards for four feet before he thudded down on to the dirt deader than a still-born calf.

For what seemed to Devlin like minutes, Warton stood where he was, the smoke cleared from his sideiron and Devlin watched as his thumb lifted the hammer again.

'You saw what happened, Sheriff,' Hal said. 'The boy drew on me and fired first. I had no option.'

Devlin fought to close his mouth before he answered. His tongue stuck to the roof of his parched mouth and he knew that any minute he was going to wet his pants.

He swallowed, trying to get non-existent saliva

that would enable him to answer the man who had a loaded gun still drawn.

'Fair fight, mister. I saw the whole thing. You had no choice.'

Devlin hadn't taken his eyes off Hal's weapon and inwardly he breathed a sigh of relief as the hammer was slowly lowered and the gun re-holstered.

'That's right, Sheriff. I had no choice.' Devlin grinned again, took out a match and flicked it with his thumb to re-light the cigar still clenched between his teeth.

Devlin took his hat off and reached for a neckerchief in his pocket. Hal's gun was out quicker than the blink of an eye.

'Jus' getting a cloth out, is all,' Devlin said, his voice about to give out on him altogether.

Hal shoved his gun back in its holster, the grin still on his face as he watched the fat man wipe the sweat from his face.

'Need me some grub,' Hal said. 'Anywhere's you recommend, Sheriff ?'

'Sure, sure. Over to the café in the hotel. Best breakfast in town. Jus' tell 'em I sent you along. They'll take real good care o' you.'

'Thanks, Sheriff, 'preciate that.' Warton winked at the sheriff and walked towards him. As he came up to Devlin he stopped: 'An', Sheriff ?'

'Yes, sir.'

'Don't you think you oughtta take care o' that body afore the flies come buzzin' round?'

'Yes, sir. I'll take care of it right away.'

Hal Warton strode off towards the café; nothing like killing a man to whet your appetite, he thought.

TWO

Gail Freemont was the sort of woman men desired and women envied. Having lived with her aunt in Boston after the tragic deaths of her parents, she broke free as soon as she came of age.

Gail's parents were killed in a railroad crash after their horse had bolted and tried to beat the loco to the crossing. Gail was five then, and for the next sixteen years she lived a genteel life under the auspices of her aunt.

Then her inheritance came through. Insurance and property made her one of the most sought-after women in Boston, but she craved for adventure and excitement.

The West.

She'd read in the newspapers about California, about the Indians, about the land of milk and honey – providing you survived the wagon trains, disease, pestilence and attacks by so-called savages. California, she decided, was the place she wanted to be.

Her aunt had argued for days. She wasn't old enough, she'd said. What about the men who sought her hand in Boston? Rich men, men of property?

Gail listened to all the arguments and dismissed each one in turn. Stubborn as her father had been, once her mind was made up, no one was going to persuade her otherwise.

The weeks of suffering on the wagon train had almost changed her mind for her. They weren't attacked by Indians – that would have been an almost welcome relief – instead, illness, heat, bugs, dust and discomfort had filled each and every day of the six-week trip.

She watched as healthy people died – some of illness, others in accidents – she nursed children and adults alike until she thought she'd scream.

On reaching California, the first layover had been Tumbleweed which was then a thriving cattle and relay station. She felt the excitement of the town lift her spirits to such an extent that she decided then and there, Tumbleweed was going to be home – at least for the time being.

That had been four years ago, and she was still there. A small house, neat and tidy with vegetable garden and barn on the outskirts of town, was her pride and joy as was the café she'd had built and ran herself. The eating habits of the whole community changed once she opened her front doors for business and, although the work was long and hard, cooking in temperatures that could melt lead, she enjoyed it.

What made every man in Tumbleweed fall under her charms was her clear, blue, wide eyes, her flashing smile and long auburn hair – not to mention a figure you'd die for and a bank balance that was healthier than a jack-rabbit in season.

From the front window of the café, Gail watched as the wagon made its way slowly down Main. A tarpaulin covered the back, but a pair of boots was easily visible as it passed by.

She'd heard the gunshots, but thought nothing of it. There hadn't been a mad panic of townspeople running to see what had happened, so Gail, like everyone else, assumed it was someone practising.

She removed her apron and headed for the front door. Tom Devlin, astride a horse that had seen better days, was level with the café as she made her way along the sidewalk.

'What's happened, Tom?' she asked.

'Stranger killed Frankie,' Devlin replied. 'It was a fair fight, I was there. Frankie got too big for his boots.'

'Oh, God.' Gail put her hands to her face. Although not overly-fond of the dead man, she nevertheless felt saddened by his untimely death.

Tom Devlin rode on; he had to speak to Jake Evans, the undertaker, make sure he took care of things properly.

Gail watched both wagon and rider until they disappeared. It had been a few months since trouble had hit Tumbleweed, two killed in a bar-room brawl that started out with fists and ended up with guns, and she was getting used to the peace.

She walked back inside the café and closed the door behind her, hoping this wasn't the start of something bad.

The café was empty but Gail knew that pretty soon, people would be queuing up for one of her famous breakfasts and, with only Molly in the kitchen, she'd better get going or they'd never be ready in time.

She entered the kitchen and was just about to refill the water butt when the bell on the front door tinkled as someone entered.

Hal Warton closed the door behind him and sat at a table set by the window. He leaned back on his chair and placed his boots on the gingham tablecloth.

'You want serving, mister, you'll put your feet where they belong,' Gail said, hands on hips and an aggressive look on her face. 'This isn't a saloon!'

Warton stared at her long and hard, a grin twitching the left hand side of his mouth. Slowly, he removed his boots from the table and sat upright.

'Happy?' he asked.

'Thank you,' Gail replied. 'Now, what'll it be?'

'Coffee, ham, eggs, bread an' whatever,' Warton said fishing for a cigar.

'I'll do you breakfast then,' Gail said and went back to the kitchen. Within minutes, the unmistakable smell of cigar smoke filtered into the room, mingling with the cooking smells.

'Damn smelly things,' Gail said under her breath.

'Oh, I dunno, I kinda like a man who smokes a cigar,' Molly said almost wistfully.

The two women prepared the breakfast and, armed with plate and coffee pot, Molly offered to serve, her curiosity getting the better of her.

'Go on then,' Gail said and stood aside to let Molly past.

'Breakfast, mister,' Molly said, flashing a smile as wide as the Grand Canyon and just as colourful.

'Thanks, ma'am,' Warton said and, without further ado, set about demolishing the food.

Molly stood for a few moments, but it was obvious the man was more interested in eating than in her; she humphed, turned on her heel, and went back to the kitchen.

'That was quicker than I expected,' Gail said, grinning.

'More interested in eating than me,' Molly said and set about washing up the pots and pans in readiness for the next meal. 'Sure is a good-looker, though,' Molly added. 'Pale, too.'

Gail laughed and they started preparing the food for the early morning rush.

* * *

Jim Warren stood looking down at his kid brother. He'd never been close to the boy, but kin was kin. Frankie had been all the kin he'd had; now that was gone.

'How'd it happen, Sheriff?' he asked Devlin.

'Frankie went for his gun,' Devlin replied. 'Guess he wasn't as quick as he thought he was.'

'Who did it?'

'Stranger, rode in last night, don't know who he is. Spent the night over to Miss Lucy's place.' Devlin spat into the spittoon on the floor by Jake Evans' desk.

'Well, I aim to find out,' Jim said and covered up the face of his dead brother.

'I don't want no trouble, Jim,' Devlin said.

'You already got trouble,' Jim replied and left the undertaker's.

Jim Warren worked out of the Triple Bar D ranch, just three miles outside town. He'd ramrodded, roped and cow-punched for most of his life and as far as he was concerned, he'd be doing that 'til the pine box came for him.

As a youth, he'd wanted his own ranch, but that was never going to be. To own a ranch you had to be either rich or lucky and Jim Warren was neither.

Jim got no reply from Lucy Montgomery's house so he headed over to the café. He'd take a look at this stranger and grab a coffee at the same time. Mourning or not, he reasoned, a man had to drink.

Hal Warton was on his third cup of coffee as Jim came in. Warton didn't even raise his head as the man entered, instead he lit a fresh cigar, sending clouds of blue smoke into the air.

Jim Warren sat at a table at the back of the café, next to the door to the kitchen and behind Warton.

He studied the man's broad back, thick black hair and cut-down holster that hung by his right hip.

Only one reason a man cut his holster down, Jim thought, and that was to draw quicker than the next man.

Gail served his food and Jim ate in silence, Warton finished eating and as he put his fork down, he threw a couple of dollars on the table and left the café.

It was at that moment that Jim suddenly realized he'd seen this man before. A long, long time ago. For the life of him he couldn't put a name to the face. But he would.

Warton walked back down Main and checked his horse out. He'd had enough of this town for a while. Besides, he thought, the people he wanted didn't live *in* Tumbleweed. They were scattered around its outskirts. Fat, rich men. Rich off the backs of the likes of him.

But he'd get his revenge. He knew that.

Mounting up, he took a long look round town as if memorizing every facet, then dug his heels into his animal's flanks and galloped off.

From the door of the café, Jim Warren watched the man go, his brain racing to remember who he was. One thing for sure, Hal Warton wasn't the name he'd been born with.

* * *

Deke Slater was fifty, and rich. Very rich. Not all his money was from ill-gotten gain, but the sums that were had started him off and although he was a law-abiding citizen now, well, for most of the time, as a young man in Texas, he'd been as wild as they came.

Drink and women could have been his downfall, as could the gambling and the shooting and the rustling, but he'd survived. Deke Slater was nothing if not a survivor.

Sitting at his desk in the house that dominated the Triple Bar D, Deke Slater finished his accounts and made his way to the kitchen where breakfast, as always, would be waiting.

Still relatively slim for his age, Deke was proud of his fitness, riding most of his hired help into the saddle at times. Deke had to win. Didn't matter what it was, Deke set out to better the next man – by fair means or foul.

He'd built his empire up on the backs of the less fortunate in the district. Squeezing them out one by one like pips from an orange until he owned all the land he'd wanted. And that was *all* the land in these parts.

There were two other ranches in the near vicinity, Jed Temper's place the Crow's Nest, and Will Harley's ranch the Circle C. Deke had no truck with either man, neither had he any desire for their land. It was too close to the hills to be of much use to Deke and his cattle ranch; he'd left them alone, meeting occasionally on a social level at first, then enlisting their help as he'd squeezed out the smaller farmers, paying for their time, of course.

Now that Deke had everything he wanted, well almost, he ignored the two men who'd helped build his little empire. The object of his desire now, and had been these past four years, was Gail Freemont. He wouldn't rest until she shared his bed; trouble was she wasn't interested in him – or anyone else for all he knew – and there was no one who'd be able to help him achieve his goal.

The hammering on the front door brought Deke back to the present and he altered course to answer it.

Through the stained glass window panel of the door he saw the tall, dark man. He didn't see the muzzle flash, but he sure felt the slug enter his chest and throw him backwards down the hallway.

He landed with a crash on the imported rug, blood spewing from the hole in his upper chest. He was more in shock than pain. But the pain came. Waves of it. Then he blacked out.

Pandemonium reigned in the household. A rider was sent off to town to get the doc, four other men saddled up to try and track down the shooter, while several more carried Deke up to his bed and laid him out.

From the blood on his back, the men guessed the slug had passed clean through, but then again, they weren't medical men. Stripping off Deke's waistcoat and shirt, the men retired as Mrs Wiggs, the housekeeper-cum-cook-cum-everything else tried to staunch the flow of blood in an effort to keep her boss alive until Doc

Williams arrived, then he'd be responsible for
Deke.

Most of the bleeding was internal and Mrs
Wiggs knew that if the old doc didn't arrive pretty
soon, Deke Slater would drown in his own blood.

Deke coughed and a trickle of blood ran down
his chin, but he was still unconscious, and Mrs
Wiggs thanked God for small mercies.

Carl Wilton, the ranch foreman, stood by the
side of Deke's bed waiting for him to regain
consciousness. He was hoping that Deke would be
able to tell him who'd shot him. Carl wasn't sure
whether he'd kill the man or shake him by the
hand.

Doc Williams arrived and after ordering towels
and hot water, ushered both Carl and Mrs Wiggs
from the room. As Deke was still unconscious, he
decided to make sure the slug was out. Rolling
Deke on to his side, he studied the exit hole,
prodding and poking with a scalpel, but there
seemed to be nothing there. He called out for Carl,
who was waiting outside.

'Carl, have a hunt round the hall, see if 'n you
can find the slug. That'll save me a whole mess o'
work and a whole deal o' pain for Deke.'

'Sure thing, Doc,' Carl said and went downstairs.
It took him ten minutes to find, and then dig out of
the woodwork, the slug that had passed through
Deke Slater.

He took it up to Doc Williams and the doc
breathed a sigh of relief. 'Good, now all I gotta do
is make sure there's no major damage, an' sew

him up. He should be as good as new come fall.'

'Well, can't win 'em all,' Carl said and left the room.

* * *

Hal Warton was already four miles from town. He knew where he was going next – to see an old friend, an old *ex*-friend – he corrected himself. Friends stick by you, they don't desert you in your hour of need.

Yes, sir, Hal thought. Good ol' Will Harley sure is gonna be surprised when he claps eyes on me.

Hal laughed out loud, but only the cactus heard him.

THREE

Jim Warren entered the café as Gail was clearing the tables. He hadn't ordered yet and he hadn't been asked.

'You know that man, Miss Freemont?' Jim asked.

'No. Never seen him before. Why?'

'He's the one jus' killed Frankie,' Jim said in a voice that almost sounded indifferent, but Gail knew otherwise.

'Oh, Jim, I'm so sorry about your brother.'

'Yeah. Sure, you an' me both. Got the feeling I know that fella, though,' Jim said and sat at a table.

'Breakfast?'

'Naw, coffee'll do, thanks.'

Gail left to fetch the coffee as Tom Devlin entered.

'He left town yet?' Devlin asked without any preamble.

'Yeah. Jus' watched him leave,' Jim replied.

'Good riddance, too,' Devlin said and sat uninvited at the same table.

'Coffee, Sheriff?' Gail asked.

'Please.'

'You recognize that man, Tom?' Jim asked.

'Nope. Never seen him afore, hope I never see him agen.'

'You keep them Wanted posters?' Jim asked.

'Sure. Got a whole drawer full of 'em,' Devlin said. 'Thanks,' he said as Gail handed him a cup of coffee.

'Mind if I go though 'em?'

'Hell no, help yourself.'

Jim Warren drained his cup and tossed a coin on the table. 'Think I'll check 'em out now. Office open?'

'Always is,' Devlin said, not offering to help in any way.

'Right. Catch you later.'

Jim Warren walked up Main to the sheriff's office. He saw no one on the way. The town seemed deserted for some reason. Folks keeping to themselves.

As usual, the sheriff's office door was unlocked. It had been a few months now since any one had been held in the single cell – even then it had been a drunk and disorderly. Jim Warren opened the bottom drawer of the wooden filing cabinet and lifted out a pile of Wanted posters. Looking at the bottom ones first he noticed they went back nearly seven years.

Jim began the painstaking task of looking through every single sheet. He didn't rightly know what he was looking for, but he sure hoped something jumped out and refreshed his memory.

* * *

Will Harley didn't even see the fist as it thudded into the side of his chin. Knocked off his feet, he hit the wall, bounced off a side table and landed on the carpet of his own hallway.

'What the –' he started, rubbing his chin.

'Howdy, Will,' Hal Warton said as he stood over the stricken man, Colt held steady as a rock aimed right between the eyes.

'Who the hell are you, mister?' Will said.

'I'll get to that later, Will. Right now I need a place to stay, some food and no more questions. *Comprende*?'

Will Harley nodded mutely, he wasn't a man who took risks, he always waited for his time to come.

'Good.' Hal kept his Colt levelled at Will's face. 'Anyone else round here?'

Again, Will shook his head. 'No one here 'til sundown. Cook's day off.'

'Perfect, Will. Jus' perfect. Now let's go through to the kitchen. Nice an' easy.'

* * *

Tom Devlin sat in the café and lingered over his coffee. Not that he was savouring every mouthful, the fact that the stranger had spent the night at Lucy's place and Jim hadn't been able to get a reply was playing on his mind.

Not the quickest of thinkers, it had taken nearly thirty minutes for this message to sink in. Now Devlin was trying to think of all the reasons under the sun why he shouldn't pay Lucy Montgomery a visit.

He couldn't think of a one.

Paying for his coffee, he said goodbye to Gail and left the café.

The sun was high in the cloudless blue sky and the heat beat down remorselessly as Devlin made his way slowly towards the Montgomery place.

There seemed to be an air of impending doom hovering over Tumbleweed. Normally, at this hour of the day, there'd be traffic on Main: women, mainly, shopping, gossiping after the early morning chores. One or two old-timers would be seeking the shade of porches, lighting up a pipe or cigar and spend most of the day watching the world pass by.

Today was different. It seemed the whole town had stayed indoors, out of harm's way.

On reaching Lucy's house, Devlin climbed the three stops to the front porch and stopped. He took his Stetson off, brushed away the dust, wiped the leather inner band, and put it back on. He hitched up his gunbelt, scratched his ear, turned, looked down Main – still deserted – took a step forwards and knocked, lightly, on the front door.

There was no reply.

Devlin stood there, confused. He wanted to turn his back and walk away, maybe even head for the saloon and chew the breeze with Slim for a while. But he knew he shouldn't.

He knocked again, louder this time. Still nothing. Placing his hands either side of his face to shield his eyes from the sunlight, he peered through the glass pane on the front door.

He couldn't believe his eyes. He blinked, rubbed his face and looked through the glass again.

There was Lucy Montgomery, large as life and naked as the day she was born, sitting in a chair not five feet from the front door. Devlin grinned and licked his lips. It'd been a long time since he'd gone with her, maybe today, he thought, he'd grab himself a piece of her ass.

Grinning, the bulge between his legs growing bigger, he took off his hat and pulled the front door towards him.

Maybe if he'd thought with what little brain he had, he'd've wondered why Lucy Montgomery was sitting there stark naked and not moving.

But Tom Devlin was only interested in one thing. He didn't notice the string strung out from the inside door knob to the trigger guard of the Winchester rifle that nestled under Lucy's left armpit.

The gun exploded in an ear shattering din that took Tom Devlin by surprise.

He actually stood and watched the small flames and smoke belch out of the barrel, saw the slug fly through the air towards his face and felt it as it sliced through the soft flesh of his cheek in an upwards spiral, shattering his cheekbone and then entering the soft pulp of his brain.

He eyes were still fixed on the ruby-red nipples

of Lucy Montgomery as he was flung backwards, down the steps and on to the soft earth of Main Street.

Tom Devlin's brain and the back of his skull flew a little further than the rest of him, coming to rest on the boardwalk on the opposite side of the street.

The shot broke through the still air of Tumbleweed like a clap of thunder. Within seconds, drapes twitched in windows, half-hidden faces peered out through dust-encrusted glass as the fat body of their sheriff came to rest.

It was Jim Warren who reached the scene first. Colt .45 held steady in his right hand, he rested on one knee beside Devlin. He didn't need to try and find a pulse to know the man was dead.

One or two people began milling about either side of Lucy's house, not coming forward, not offering any assistance.

'Anyone see anythin'?' Warren yelled, never taking his eyes off Lucy's front door.

No one said a word or even bothered to shake their head.

Warren stood and, half crouched, made his way towards the open door. Whoever had killed Devlin, he thought, might still be in there.

Sweat broke out on his forehead and ran in tiny streams down towards his eyebrows, then through them, trying to drip into his eyes and blind him.

He quickly dragged his left arm across his forehead, wiping the sweat away without obscuring his vision.

Jim Warren climbed the steps to the porch. He

stood to one side of the open door in case whoever was in there tried to blow *his* brains out. He peered round the opening. Inside, the hallway was in comparative darkness and he paused, letting his eyes grow accustomed to the gloom.

Then he saw Lucy.

She sat on a chair, legs spread, rifle tied under her right side and scarf that was a mite too tight round her neck. Her face was puffy and blue-black, her swollen tongue hung lifelessly from her grotesquely painted mouth.

Warren almost gagged.

There was a smell. A smell Jim Warren both feared and hated. It was the smell of death.

He saw the string, he saw where it went and he reholstered his own gun. The door had been booby-trapped. Lucy Montgomery was dead and, whoever had killed her wasn't content with that death.

'Someone git the doc,' Warren shouted.

Reluctantly, one of the bystanders ambled down Main towards Doc Williams' place. The man was in no hurry. No need.

Jim Warren removed his hat and entered the house. He grabbed a coat that hung just as lifelessly as Lucy from a wooden coat-stand and placed it over Lucy's body. She may have been a whore, he thought, but he didn't want everyone gawping at her. She had a right to *some* dignity.

He stared at her swollen face, forcing himself to take in every detail. Then he looked at the scarf that had killed her.

It was tied so tight, the soft material had actually cut through the flesh of her neck and, from the lump that stuck out to one side, Jim knew her neck bone had been broken.

It was then he rushed outside and threw up in front of everyone assembled there.

But he didn't care. Wiping his mouth, he stood guard over the front door, waiting for Doc Williams to arrive.

'I'll be danged,' a man called from the opposite side of the street. 'If 'n this ain't the back o' Devlin's head!'

Warren shifted his gaze to the moron who was crouched down on his haunches, poking the blood and gore that littered the boardwalk.

Warren drew his gun and, feeling a need to release pent-up emotion, he fired twice into the air.

What he'd really wanted to do was shoot the idiot. But his commonsense prevailed – just.

'Git outta here,' Warren yelled hoarsely. 'Git outta here!'

Quickly, quicker than most of the townsfolk were used to moving, they melted back into their wooden shacks, closing the doors behind them. The street was empty once again, save for Jim and Tom Devlin's body of course.

'He ain't there,' a voice called out.

'Who ain't?' Warren asked.

'The doc. There ain't no one home.'

'Shit!' What the hell was Jim Warren supposed to do? he wasn't sheriff, not even a deputy. He was a ranch-hand, pure and simple. this wasn't his problem, or was it?

In that split second, Jim Warren *knew* it was his problem.

Although he had no evidence, he knew who'd killed Lucy and who'd set the booby-trap.

Gail Freemont left the café, she was carrying a blanket and she reverently laid it over the body of Tom Devlin.

'I'll get Jake,' she said. 'He'll take care of Tom and Lucy.'

In spite of his feelings, Jim smiled at Gail. 'Thanks,' he managed to say. 'Thanks.'

FOUR

'That's the best I can do for now,' Doc Williams said, repacking his black bag and wiping the blood from his hands with a clean rag.

'Thanks, Doc,' Mrs Wiggs said. 'I can take care of him now.'

'I'm sure you can. I'm sure you can. Anyone see who shot him?' Doc asked.

'No. The shot came through the door, Mr Slater never even opened it,' one of the men said.

'Better inform the sheriff when I get back to town,' Doc Williams stood up. He was young for a doctor, thirty-three. Born and raised in Tumbleweed, his parents, now dead, wanted their only son to become a medical man, and had worked their fingers to the bone to send him through medical school.

Dan Williams graduated the day after his parents died. He never did find out what killed them, and about twelve other folks in and around Tumbleweed, but took it upon himself to make sure that Tumbleweed had a doctor.

Taking an offered glass of whiskey, Dan took

his leave, loaded up his buggy, and set off for Tumbleweed.

Deke Slater, more comfortable now in his own bed, propped up with pillows, was looking forward to being spoiled rotten by his housekeeper. Breathing was a little difficult, but at least he felt no pain, unless he moved, and he planned to do little of that for the next few days.

The ride back to town was uneventful and Doc Williams unhitched his bay mare, fed and watered her, and then made his way into his study. The first thing he always did after being called out to any case was write up a report; he never knew when what he wrote would come in handy. Medicine, still in its infancy, was a continual learning process and Doc Williams was hungry to learn more.

The knock on his front door was, therefore, annoying. Annoying, that is, until he saw who stood outside on his porch.

He might be the doc, but he was also a man and the sight of Gail Freemont set his heart fit to bust.

'Dan, I'm sorry to disturb you, but there's been a double killing in town,' Gail said, flushing slightly at the direct look Dan was giving her.

'Who's dead?' Dan asked.

'Lucy and Sheriff Devlin.'

'Good God!' Anyone see anything?'

'Dan, this is Tumbleweed. Remember? I got Jake to take the bodies over to the mortuary, in case you wanted to have a look.'

'Thanks, Gail. I'll come right away.'

Without even bothering to don his jacket, Dan walked across town with Gail. All he could think about was asking Gail out for dinner, but he knew this was neither the time nor the place.

He thanked her – for what he knew not – and watched as she made her way back to the café.

Shaking his head to clear the thoughts that refused to leave of their own accord, Dan knocked on Jake Evans' door.

After a few moments, the door opened a fraction and the beady eyes and nose of the town undertaker eyed up his visitor. As soon as he saw who it was, the door opened fully and Dan couldn't help noticing Jake replace the Winchester he'd been holding.

'Jake,' Dan said. 'Mite nervous today.'

'Hell, Dan. Two folks dead already, I don't aim to make it a trio.'

Dan smiled. Jake Evans was a cagey old customer. His hobby was making the dead look more alive than when they *were* alive. Even drifters were made up by Jake, blusher on the cheeks, male or female, lipstick, likewise.

His favourite occupation was putting the dead back together again – before he buried them.

'Through here, Dan,' Jake said, leading the way to a back room that contained two tables – and two bodies. He never thought to mention the third body he'd collected earlier in the day.

'Cause of death, Jake?' Dan asked.

'Strangulation, some evidence o' sexual inty-course, but it's Lucy, so 'nuff said. Tom here's had the back o' his head blowed off. I scooped it up off 'n the sidewalk. It's yonder in the bucket. Aim to fix him up a right treat when you've done.'

Dan lifted the sheet from Lucy Montgomery's head. Jake was correct. The black face and swollen tongue and eyeballs out on sticks were obvious to anyone. He replaced the sheet and lifted the one covering Tom Devlin.

The small, neat round hole in Tom's cheek, almost bloodless, belied the hideous exit wound the slug had left in its wake.

'Cheap bullet,' Jake said.

'What makes you say that?' Dan asked.

'Not weighted properly. Probably home-made. Looks to me like the lead split after it bounced off the cheekbone, that's how come nearly the whole of the back o' Tom's head is a'missing.'

'You don't miss much, Jake,' Dan said almost admiringly.

'Hell, seen enough bullet wounds in my time,' Jake said matter-of-factly.

'Guess you have, Jake.'

'I'll fix 'em up and crate 'em away,' Jake said, 'assuming you've finished.'

'Nothing I can do for them,' Dan agreed. 'I guess the funeral of Tom will be met by the Town Council?'

'Reckon so,' Jake said, already relishing the prospect of fixing the jig-saw of Tom's skull back into place.

'I'll go see Ted, he's acting mayor, isn't he?'

'Actin's the right word for it.'

Dan smiled and left Jake to his creations. Outside, he ran across Jim Warren.

'Doc! Thought you was out o' town,' Jim said shaking Dan's hand.

'I was. Someone tried to kill Deke Slater.'

'Deke dead?'

'No. Hit pretty bad, but he'll survive.'

'What the hell's goin' on,' Jim said almost to himself. 'Three killin's already and it ain't even noon yet.'

'Three?'

'Yeah. Stranger killed my brother, Frankie, first light this mornin'.'

'I'm sorry, Jim. I didn't know.'

'Makes no difference,' Jim said. 'Nothin' you could've done, anyways.'

'These killings linked, Jim?'

'Seems to me they are. Stranger comes to town, and within a day, three people are dead an' one injured.'

'Motive?'

'Hell, beats me. I'm just goin' back to the sheriff's office to continue looking through the Wanted posters. See if 'n I can throw any light on the subject.'

'We don't have a sheriff or a deputy then?'

'Nope.'

'I'll call by later, Jim,' Dan said. 'I'm just off to see Ted over at the hardware store. It's his turn to be mayor.'

The two men grinned at each other and went about their business.

* * *

The news of the recent killings quickly spread around both the town and outlying districts. Riders from the three main ranches, staying over after a night of drinking, spread the word.

Jed Temper, boss of the Crow's Nest ranch found out about it from one of his own hands. It didn't take Jed long to put two and two together.

A ghost from the long and distant past. That's what he thought, he was convinced of it. But what to do? Deke was out of commission, and Tom Devlin dead. That left Will Harley and himself, the only two fit survivors of that night long, long ago.

Jed Temper had moved to Tumbleweed over thirty years ago. A sailor, he'd got fed up with the rigours of the ocean and decided to make landfall – for good – hence the unusual name of his ranch.

It had been a long and hard transition until the arrival of Harley and Slater, then things became easier – much easier. The town sheriff had been deposed and Devlin had replaced him. Devlin, a fat tub of lard, was frightened of his own shadow, so frightened, in fact, he'd learned to keep his mouth shut. In return, he'd been sheriff of Tumbleweed ever since. Until now, that is.

Jed made up his mind to ride over to the Circle C and tell Will Harley what he thought was happening. No, what he *knew* was happening.

But he'd wait 'til nightfall. He didn't want to create any suspicion, it was well known that he, Deke and Will did *not* get along too well.

Something they'd all agreed upon all those years ago.

Yeah, he thought, I'll wait 'til nightfall.

* * *

'Seems to me we need a new sheriff,' Ted Wilmont said without looking up and without stopping loading up his shelves with fresh provisions brought in by the stage the night before.

'Any likely candidates?' Dan asked.

'None as I can think of,' Ted answered.

'What about Jim Warren?'

'Frankie's brother?'

'Yes.'

'He's working out at Deke's place, ain't he?'

'He was. He's been in town all mornin', on account of Frankie's death. He's over at the sheriff's office now, checking through Wanted posters.'

'Wanted posters?'

'Yes. Seems to think the stranger that killed Frankie might have more than a passing interest in the deaths of Tom and Lucy – come to think of it, he might even be involved in the shooting of Deke.'

'Jim recognize the fella?' Ted asked.

'Not that I know,' Dan replied.

'Mmmm.'

'What's that supposed to mean?'

'Nothin', jus' thinkin' over your suggestion, is all.'

'Can't think of anyone else in town who'd be willing – or indeed – able to be sheriff,' Dan said.

'You wanna have a word with Jim?' Ted asked.

'If you want me to.'

' 'Preciate it.'

'Okay. I'll go see him.'

Dan found Jim sitting in Devlin's old chair, surrounded by Wanted posters – some so old they were almost brown.

'Anything, Jim?' Dan asked.

'Nope. Not a thing. Seems like there's two, maybe three years I can't find.'

'Thought Tom kept 'em all,' Dan said, taking a chair opposite the single cell door.

'Well, 'less he's put 'em someplace else, looks like he's tossed 'em.'

'Jim, I've just had a word with Ted Wilmont. As you know, we don't have any law enforcement in town any more and we were wonderin'—'

'Now jus' hang on there,' Jim Warren said. 'I'm two steps ahead of yer.'

'Well?'

'I don't know nothin' 'bout bein' sheriff. All I know is ranchin'. There must be someone else who's more qualified than I am.'

'There isn't anyone who's got more motivation, Jim.'

Jim Warren thought about that. Dan Williams was right. If he didn't track down this man or at least try and discover his motives, let alone if he was responsible for the killings of Tom and Lucy – well then he wasn't the man he thought he was.

Devlin's words kept going over and over in his head: *It was a fair fight, Jim.*

'Okay. I'll do it. Leastways, I'll give it my best shot.'

Dan stood and held his hand out. 'Congratulations, Sheriff. I'll get Ted over, he can swear you in, all legal an' above board.'

'Yeah. Right.' Jim was already back to his hunt through the Wanted posters.

FIVE

'An' by the power invested in me by the Governor of the State of California, etc, etc, you's the sheriff. Congratulations, Jim, here's your tin star.'

'Thanks, Ted. I don't know if I'm gonna be any good as sheriff, but I'll give it my best shot,' Jim said as he fixed the star to his vest.

'Can't ask no more'n that, Jim,' Ted Wilmont slapped Jim on the back and then shook his hand. 'Well, I got me a store to run. Catch you later.'

'See you, Ted,' Jim said but the man had already closed the door behind him.

'Well, Sheriff. How does it feel?' Dan asked.

'Hell, no dif'rent 'cept the star,' Jim Warren said, staring down at his chest.

'Any luck with the Wanted posters?'

'Not yet, but then, I ain't bin through 'em all.'

'I'll leave you to get on, Jim. If you want anything, you know where I am,' Dan said and he, too, left the office.

Jim Warren sat down behind *his* desk and rested his booted feet on it. He stared around the small office, making a mental note of its contents:

desk, two chairs, wood-stove, gun rack and ammo store, both locked, coffee pot, two battered tin mugs, a filing cabinet and a hat stand.

Jim stood and walked towards the small door set at the back of the office; walking through it, he saw, not for the first time, the single cell. Wooden bars, a bunk and that was it.

Jim smiled to himself, many's the night he'd spent on that small, uncomfortable cot, rather than ride back to the ranch, never arrested, but a free bed.

By the dirt and dust on the floor of the cell, Jim could tell no one had occupied that cot for a long time, even the keys were hanging limply in the metal lock.

Jim took them out and hung them on his belt. He might need them before too long.

He returned to the desk and pored over the Wanted posters once more. He stayed, unmoving for the next hour, until his eyeballs felt as if they were out on stalks.

The various artists' impressions of killers, rustlers, bank robbers, stagecoach robbers, all seemed to look the same and Jim decided it was time for a rest.

He left the office and walked across to Gail's café, coffee was what he needed.

Entering the café, he sat at the table opposite the large front window; better to keep his eye on Main, after all, he was sheriff now.

He sat trying to work out his next move. Without a motive, Jim reasoned, he could hardly raise a posse – if indeed Tumbleweed was capable of raising a posse – and ride hell for leather after this Hal Warton critter.

The only witness to Frankie's shooting was now dead, but Devlin had told him it was a fair fight.

There were no witnesses – at least no one would come forward – to the killings of either Lucy or Tom.

Maybe he should ride out to Triple Bar D and have a word with Deke Slater, he thought. He'd have to tell Deke he wouldn't be around the ranch for a while now he was sheriff anyway.

Molly brought out a mug and the pot and left them on the table for Jim. She smiled at him and he smiled back, but he couldn't help noticing that young Molly smiled at him a mite friendlier than usual. Being sheriff could have unexpected perks.

Draining the last of his coffee, he made his mind up to visit Deke, see if anything could shed some light on what was going on, for, he reasoned, so far he had diddlyswot!

Jim stood and threw some coins on the tabletop, Molly came in from the kitchen and picked up the mug and pot and Jim couldn't help noticing how pretty she was. He also couldn't help noticing how close she stood by him as she cleared the table.

'See you later, Sheriff,' she said almost coyly.

'You sure will, Molly. You sure will.'

'I hope so,' she said and smiled again and Jim felt his heart go all aflutter.

He tipped his hat and left, feeling Molly's eyes burning into the back of his head. Once outside, he took a few deep breaths to calm himself down. He had to concentrate on the job in hand, but later, maybe? He couldn't help smiling to himself.

The livery stable was deserted, so again, he left some coins in the metal plate set by the stalls and saddled up his mount. He checked his sideiron, then pulled the Winchester from its scabbard and made sure that that, too, was fully loaded.

Satisfied, he mounted up and walked the mare out into the heat of the day, heading west to the Triple Bar D and Deke Slater.

* * *

Dan Williams was becoming restless. Things didn't seem to add up anymore. There was something going on, or had gone on, in and around Tumbleweed, and he hadn't a clue what it was.

Maybe he'd led a blinkered existence? Maybe it was time he did a bit of investigating himself? But where to start and what would he be looking for?

The more he thought about the town, the more he began to realize that since his return, nearly three years ago, there *had* been an uncomfortable atmosphere round the place.

Granted, he'd been at medical school for six years, and in that time had only returned once, and that very briefly. So most of the folks he'd known as a youth had either died or moved on.

Died! For no reason whatsoever, Dan's thoughts had turned to his parents.

When he'd received the wire telling him of their

deaths, he'd taken the details of their demise as gospel.

Fever, sickness, death. He'd returned for the funerals a week after graduating, but had not seen the bodies – had not wished to see them.

The cemetery had been packed with folks, there had been seven people to bury that day, he remembered, and it seemed to pass him by like a nightmare. All he wanted to do was get home and be on his own.

The town had been in mourning for a week afterwards, sympathetic glances dogged his footsteps until he felt he had to do something. That's why he'd set up a practice here.

In his singlemindedness, he'd never queried the dozen or so deaths, maybe he would have done had his own mother and father been just two of the twelve. But now, now he felt it was time to take a closer look.

The town meeting hall, he decided was the best place to start. Town records, maybe even newspapers of the day could prove useful starting points. Besides, there wasn't much going on in town at the moment. No babies due and, apart from Deke Slater, no one else needing his ministration.

Dan made his mind up and left his surgery feeling quite excited at the prospect of turning up something that might provide a clue to these mysterious killings.

*   *   *

Through the heat-haze, Jim Warren saw the large entrance to the Triple Bar D straight ahead. The hot breeze made the sign hanging atop the the poles swing back and forth in a rhythmic, squeaky fashion, the sunlight reflecting off the bright red paint.

Lower down, nailed to one of the uprights, was another sign:

NO TRESSPASSIN

Jim smiled, no one had remembered to add the 'G' to the sign yet. He rode on down the trail and straight up the over-large ranch house that Deke had built nigh on three years ago.

Several hands waved as they saw Jim approach, one or two walked over to him as he dismounted and hitched his mare to the pole outside the house.

'You're wearin' a star!' one of the men said.

'Yup.'

'You foolin' us?'

'Nope.'

'Goddamn it to hell an' back. You the sheriff now?'

'Yup.'

Jim walked up the steps and knocked on the front door; while he waited for it to open he turned and grinned at the ranch hands that stood looking up at him.

'You boys be good, now,' he said just as Mrs Wiggs opened the front door.

'Jim Warren, what are you doin' a-knocking on the door?'

'G'day, Mrs Wiggs, I've come to have a few words with Deke. He up?'

'No, he ain't up. The man's bin shot, didn't you know that?'

'Yeah, that's why I'm here, I need to ask him a few questions,' Jim said politely.

'Don't know if 'n he's up be bein' asked questions, *Sheriff*,' Mrs Wiggs pointed the last word as if in disapproval.

'Be grateful if you could ask him, Mrs Wiggs,' Jim said.

'Wait there.' She closed the front door, leaving Jim standing there like a carpetbagger

Five minutes later she returned and grudgingly told him to come in. 'But make sure them boots is clean,' she added, making sure he knew who was in charge.

Jim wiped his feet removing all the trail dust then stepped inside.

'Follow me.' Mrs Wiggs led the way through the hall and up the staircase. She stopped outside one of three mahogany doors and knocked, gently.

'Come in,' a voice bellowed that didn't sound at all sick to Jim Warren.

'Damn it to hell an' back,' Deke Slater said. 'You're wearing a badge!'

'Sure am, Mr Slater.' Jim then proceeded to tell Deke Slater all that had taken place in town that morning.

Deke's face clouded over. Jim was sure he knew

more than he was letting on. Including the identity of his own attacker.

* * *

Hal Warton was enjoying himself. The longer he kept Will Harley prisoner, the more nervous the man became.

Warton was convinced that Will *still* didn't know who he was – or if he did he was sure putting on a good act.

'How long you gonna keep this up, mister?' Will said, trying his damnedest to keep his voice even.

'Don't know yet, Harley. Long as I want, the way I figure it.' Warton lit a cigar and blew a cloud of blue smoke in Harley's face.

'Min' tellin' me what you're after?' Will asked.

'Nope. I don't mind, but I ain't ready to tell – not yet. You'll find out, sooner or later. Could be the last thing you ever do learn.'

Warton left the threat hanging in the air. He'd noticed the expression on Will's face as he'd said the last sentence. Warton grinned, showing blackened teeth, those that were still in his mouth, which wasn't that many.

'Mind if I make some coffee?' Warton's tone of voice had changed completely, it was as if he were an old friend or a casual visitor.

'Seein's how I'm all trussed up like a pig goin' to market, there's no way I can stop you,' Will said defiantly.

' 'Preciate that, Will. 'Preciate that.'

Warton left the room and went outside to the pump and filled a pitcher. The wood-stove was already alight, crackling away in the corner of the kitchen. He scooped coffee into a pot, filled it with cold water and set it atop the stove. Then he resumed his seat. He just stared at Will Harley without saying a word.

But Will Harley had the fear of the devil jumping around his stomach. He realized at that moment that this stranger was going to kill him, and kill him soon.

SIX

After the early morning breakfast rush, it was Gail's habit on a Sunday to go home for a few hours and sort out the daily chores of running her own home single-handed. Leaving Molly in charge of the café, just in case they had a few late callers, Molly would stay for two, sometimes three hours before closing up for the rest of the day.

Most folks ate dinner at home on the Sabbath, and those that didn't made sure they got a big breakfast.

Apart from the killings, which Molly had kept well away from, nothing much was different that Sunday morning. The usual group of people had come and gone, one or two late starters had scuttled in just after Gail had left but Molly had soon sorted them out.

Now the café was quiet. She busied herself cleaning up the tables, brushing the floor and then washed up the dishes while she doused the stove down ready for the next day.

It suddenly occured to her that one regular, a man she could set her watch by, had not been in the café that day: Will Harley.

The more she thought about it, and considered the troubles of the morning, the more she worried.

Will Harley had looked after her when her own mother had been taken ill and her father was out on a drive. She'd become quite attached to the old man. Either he was ill, or— Molly decided to take no chances.

Quickly finishing up her chores, she locked the café and made her mind up to pay Will a visit. If he wasn't well, she'd fix him up breakfast and come back for the doc. If he was all right, then she'd have nothing to worry about.

Molly had a room over the café, she'd lived there for nearly a year. After the death of her parents, Gail had taken her on and the two women got on so well that the café flourished in a way neither of them could have imagined. A perfect partnership.

Gail's buggy was parked round back, and rather than sort her own horse out, Molly decided to borrow that. She hitched up the old mare and set off to visit Will Harley, but not before taking some biscuits and bacon and a couple of eggs with her – just in case there was no food out there.

The day was hot, as ever, and being Sunday, there weren't many people out and about. The only person she saw was Doc Williams as he entered the town hall. He didn't see her though, and maybe a lot of trouble could have been averted if he had.

Molly was glad to be out in the fresh air after

the smoke-filled kitchen and although it was a good ten miles to the Circle C, she looked upon it as a day out. She hadn't been out to the small ranch for a few months and she knew that a drive had left Tumbleweed four days ago. As was their custom, the three ranchers, Deke Slater, Will Harley and Jed Temper, teamed up when a large drive was ready to go, each man sending his own gang of five or six drovers to take care of their own brands.

The cattlemen would be away for at least six weeks, so Molly knew that, apart from Josie Wells, the widow-woman who cooked and cleaned for Will, the ranch would be almost deserted.

She decided that if Will *was* well, and had simply decided not to come into town, which was highly unlikely, she'd make a fuss of him and maybe spend a few hours in his company, then return home before sundown.

Although her thoughts were looking on the bright side, she had a funny feeling in her stomach that all was *not* well out at the Circle C.

* * *

Dan Williams, being a member of the town council and a respected member of the community, didn't have to seek permission to go through the town records.

He found copies of newspapers from as far away as Denver, Colorado, as well as San Francisco and a few from Los Angeles. For a while, he was so engrossed in reading articles and stories about those fine towns and cities that he almost forgot why he'd come in in the first place.

He had to force himself to stop reading and look for the register of births and deaths that he knew was stored here.

In all the years since the deaths of his parents, Dan had never seen fit to read the record of the death. He had no need. He had no doubts as to the cause. No suspicious circumstances, he'd taken everything at face value.

Jed Temper had been mayor and both Deke Slater and Will Harley had been on the town council. They'd only retired when Dan arrived back in town and new officers had been elected. Himself, Ted Wilmont and Jake Evans had taken over and run the town since then, not that the town *needed* running.

The fortunes of Tumbleweed were balanced with the fortunes of the three main ranches that surrounded it. When they did well, the town prospered, when the ranches suffered, either from drought or disease, the town suffered. It was in the hands of God, Dan thought, they all just went with the flow, making minor adjustments as and when necessary.

From the dust and sand that covered most of the journals and books Dan was looking through, he could tell that no one had been through the records for a long time. His own register of events in Tumbleweed, a sort of diary more than anything else, he'd kept at his surgery, along with his notes on the success and/or failure of operations he'd performed: broken legs and arms, bullet wounds, mostly. He'd also pulled a few teeth, delivered a few babies along the way, as well as tended sick calves and horses. Most folks thought a doctor was a doctor was a doctor, the fact he'd had no veterinary training was of little consequence to them.

The sound of the town hall door creaking open made him look round and there, framed in the doorway, sunlight shining all around her, stood Gail Freemont. Dan closed a book he was holding and took a deep breath. She looked as pretty as a picture.

'I thought I saw you come in here, Dan,' Gail said.

'Gail, you look lovely,' Dan said trying to cover up his embarrassment as best he could.

'I was just going for a walk, thought you might like to accompany me, if you're not *too* busy.' Gail twirled her parasol and smiled.

Dans legs melted from beneath him. He looked at the town files and then back at Gail. There was no contest.

'I'd be delighted,' he said and closed the cupboard door, locking it behind him. A twinge of guilt filled him for a few seconds, but, he reasoned, he could come back after their walk.

Dan walked towards Gail and, after holding the door for her, he closed and locked it. She put her arm through his and they set off along the boardwalk. Tumbleweed wasn't that big a place, you could walk from one end to other in a couple of minutes and Dan could see that the fine dress and polished shoes Gail was wearing were hardly suitable attire for a stroll down the trail.

'My buggy's parked round back of the café,' Gail said. 'We could always take a trip out to Black Rock Bend, it might be cooler out there, with the river and everything.'

'My pleasure,' Dan said. 'I'll just leave a note on my door – just in case.'

Pinning a note to his front door, he led Gail round to the back of the café.

'That's strange,' Gail said. 'I left the buggy here this morning.'

'Perhaps Molly's borrowed it,' Dan offered. 'Never mind, I'll hitch mine up, it'll only take a few moments.'

'I'll just check, see if Molly's here,' Gail said.

'Okay, I'll hitch up and meet you outside the café in, say, five minutes.'

'I'll be waiting, Dan,' Gail said.

Exactly five minutes later, Dan reined in his horse outside the café just as Gail was locking the front door behind her.

'Molly in?' he asked.

'No. Perhaps you're right, she's probably borrowed it to go for a ride.'

Dan jumped down from the buggy and helped Gail up on to the maroon leather seat. Dan had already pulled the sun-shade up, so Gail put her parasol down and they set off for Black Rock Bend, without a care in the world.

* * *

Pete Sidler was a stranger in Tumbleweed. For two days he'd been camped outside town, coming in in the evenings to the saloon and then disappearing again.

Young, fresh faced, he posed no threat nor evoked any comment from those who saw him. Keeping much to himself, he just watched and listened to what was going on.

He'd shared a cell with Hal Warton for the past six years. They'd formed a partnership and friendship that only men in a federal prison could do.

Ten years younger than Warton, Pete Sidler was a killer.

Standing five-feet-eight inches he was stocky, with jet black hair and eyes so deep brown they looked as black as the beard growth that covered most of his face.

He'd been captured in Tucson after trying to hold the bank up. Him and another feller, Pete couldn't quite recall his name, had been surprised by the marshal and ten deputies as they tried to make their getaway.

His pard had been killed but Pete, Pete had only been wounded.

Unknown to the marshal, Pete Sidler was wanted in four states, for murder and robbery in the main, but that information hadn't reached Arizona, so he was tried and convicted only of attempted bank robbery.

His pard, shot dead in a hail of lead, had not played the odds. All but surrounded by tin stars, Pete had raised his hands: his pard drew his gun but never even loosed off a single shot before being cut down with enough lead to cover a roof.

Hal Warton and Pete Sidler had made a pact. Warton was released three days before Pete, and had enlisted the help of his friend to carry out his plan of revenge.

He hadn't gone into every little detail, but Pete knew enough to know they'd both come out of this rich men. Very rich men.

Pete watched as Dan Williams locked the town hall doors. He watched him walk arm in arm down Main with the café woman, then he stood in an alleyway and watched as they rode out of town.

Hal was right, he thought. That Doc Williams is becoming suspicious. Hal Warton had had six long years to hatch up his plan. And, apart from rock-busting out in the desert, he'd not had a lot to take his mind off his revenge.

He'd worked out every detail; he knew the exact order in which he'd do the killings, and he knew exactly how he was going to do them.

Frankie Warren had been a bonus, but, though he didn't know he hadn't killed Deke Slater, as far as he was concerned, everything was going according to plan.

Pete Sidler was an able listener, it had almost become *his* revenge, too. When a man hasn't got anything else to think or talk about but revenge, nothing else matters.

Checking that Main was deserted, Pete set the next part of the plan in motion.

Rolling a cigarette, he struck a match on his belt-buckle and inhaled the acrid smoke. Letting the match burn away, he lit some dried grass sprouting out from beneath the weatherboards of the town hall.

It had been four months since even a shower had hit Tumbleweed. The wooden boards were drier than a steer's skeleton parched in the desert sun.

Pete didn't have to hang around checking to see if the building was afire, it almost exploded in its eagerness to burn down.

Within minutes, great tongues of flame were licking their way up the side of the building, sending sparks and ash high into the still air.

It was just as Hal had predicted: he knew that someone would go back through the town records. He sure was a smart feller, Pete thought as he mounted his horse and rode back to his temporary campsite, just the other side of Black Rock Bend.

SEVEN

From the kitchen window, Hal Warton watched as the buggy neared. Already alerted by the cloud of dust on the horizon, he'd watched as it entered Circle C land.

He couldn't make out the driver, but his Winchester was loaded, aimed and ready. The sunlight shining directly into his eyes made it impossible to see how many men were on the buggy, but he wasn't bothered. He knew he had the element of surprise, he'd just bide his time and then—

He'd gagged Will Harley so there was no way the old fool could give a warning. Hal watched and waited. He began to get a hard on, as he always did before he shot someone, killing to him was better than sex – he grinned to himself – ask Lucy Montgomery, he thought and almost said it out loud.

The buggy was only a hundred yards away now and the far barn blocked out the sunlight so Hal could see the driver.

Only one person, and a gal to boot. He licked his

lips and lowered the rifle.

'Seems you got a visitor, Will,' Hal said. He leaned the rifle against the wall and took out his Colt, cocking the hammer as he did so.

From outside, Will heard the horse come to a halt, then he heard footsteps, first as they landed on the ground, then as they climbed the steps to the porch. Then he heard the knock on the door. A soft knock and then a woman's voice:

'Will! You in there, Will?'

Hal Warton grinned and it sent a shiver of fear through Will Harley.

'Will, are you in there?' the voice called out again.

Hal stepped out of the kitchen and went to the front door. Colt levelled, he pulled the door inwards and stood there eyeballing Molly.

'Well, come on in, little lady. It was gettin' boring in here anyways,' he said as he grabbed her by the arm and dragged her inside.

He slammed the front door shut and shot the bolt.

'Where's Will?' Molly asked; fear hadn't yet got a hold, and she was more concerned about the welfare of Will.

'Never you mind about him,' Hal said, 'you got more to worry about than that old fool.'

From the kitchen, Molly heard the grunts Will was making through the gag. She dropped the basket of food she was toting and backed into the kitchen. She couldn't see any obvious signs of injury on Will, but she asked nevertheless: 'You

okay Will? What's going on? Who is this man?
Why's he got you hog-tied?'

The questions just rolled out of her mouth and
Hal Warton laughed his head off.

'He can't answer none o' them dumb questions,
little lady. He's wearing a gag!' and he laughed
some more.

'Women!' he said, wiping a tear from his eye,
'they're all the same, alus askin' dumb questions.'

'What is it you want?' Molly asked.

'Feedin', that's what I want. Now you git to
cookin' up some o' that grub you brung, an' keep
your damn mouth shut!'

Molly looked at Will and saw the imploring look
in his eyes, then she turned to face Hal Warton
and her eyes fell to his gun.

'You going to kill me?' she asked.

'Maybe. Maybe not, depends.'

'On what?'

'On how damn quick you git to cookin'!'

Molly didn't need telling twice. From the look in
the gunman's eyes, she could tell, instinctively,
that he was more than a half a canteen short.
There was a manic look about the man, and that's
when Molly first felt *real* fear.

Warton stood looking at her. Not in the eye, he
glanced over her face and she felt his eyes burn
into her body. She watched as he unashamedly
stared at her pert breasts, he licked his lips, and
then his eyes moved on down her body. Molly was
glad she was wearing jeans and not the long dress
she wore in the café. But Warton was able to see

her shapely hips and long legs and the hard-on he had was all too evident.

Molly broke away and turned her back on him, still feeling his eyes on her like red-hot needles. She felt her stomach muscles tighten as her nerves got the better of her and all the strength she'd had began to sap out of her body.

With trembling fingers she began unpacking the food basket, laying out the biscuits, eggs and ham on the table that stood next to the stove.

She reached for the large charcoal-blackened frying pan that hung on a hook over the stove; it was too heavy for one arm and she grabbed the wooden handle with both hands.

For an instant, she had a weapon. For an instant, she thought about using it, but out of the corner of her eye she saw Warton's leering face, and he was still clutching the Colt.

The instant went past her and she placed the pan on the stove, melting lard and then adding the ham and eggs.

Soon the kitchen smelled like any other ordinary kitchen, the food sizzling in the pan. Only Will and Molly didn't think about their prison as an ordinary kitchen.

*   *   *

Gail and Dan had talked almost non-stop on their way out to Black Rock Bend. After the initial embarrassment and awkward silences had passed, they talked about anything and everything.

As Gail had said, the breeze was cooler out here than in town, the sound of the water adding to a more comfortable atmosphere.

Black Rock wasn't black rock, but a huge outcrop of granite, a survivor from years long gone, when the river was much bigger.

Once surrounded by sandstone, the core was now the only rock left for miles around. The river, unable to erode the granite as easily as the sandstone, had altered course here as the level dropped, creating an ox-bow and deep pool of clear, almost stationary water that the kids of the town used for swimming. It got its name from the fact that the pool was so deep, the water *looked* black.

Parking the buggy, Dan held Gail round the waist to help her down. She placed her hands on his shoulders and, as her feet hit the ground, Dan kept his hands where they were – so did Gail.

An awkward silence enveloped them. They stared into each other's eyes, their bodies almost touching. Dan went to lean forward, but it was Gail who turned her head very slightly to say no, not yet, Dan Williams.

Dan straightened up and released her waist. Gail smiled up at him and removed her hands from his broad shoulders. The moment passed.

'Well, let's go sit by the water,' Dan said lightly, trying to overcome his acute embarrassment. No man liked being rejected, and to make him feel more comfortable, Gail linked her arm through his.

'Right, let's go,' she said, smiling up at him, seeing the hurt etched in his blue eyes.

In silence, they picked their way up the gentle incline of granite that led to the riverbed.

The rock was smooth and Dan could feel the heat of the stone burning through the leather soles of his boots. Reaching the crest, the rock then sloped down gently to the water's edge and the water was as black as Dan remembered it.

Memories came flooding back to him: his mother not wanting him to go swimming there, his father saying the boy had to learn how to take care of himself in the water, and his mother asking why? He smiled to himself.

His mother was, as all mothers are, a worrier. Two boys and a girl had drowned at Black Rock Bend. Out of their depth, and with no one to help, the three had been carried downstream, their naked bodies being washed up on Deke Slater's land.

Dan tried hard to remember their names, but he couldn't.

'This looks a good spot,' Gail said, pointing to a small rise that had a good view of the surrounding country.

'I love it out here,' Gail went on. 'When the heat of the day's too much, and the noise and dust of town become unbearable, I often come out here and just sit.

'Sometimes I dangle my feet in the water, too. Keeps you nice and cool.'

'As a child I used to come out here every day,'

Dan said. 'All us kids used to come out and swim and joke around. They were good times.'

'I wish I'd known you then,' Gail said and lowered her eyes, coyly.

'So do I,' Dan said as he sat beside her.

For a few minutes they sat in silence, staring at the water, watching the harsh sunlight reflect off the gentle ripples. On the other side of the river, the desert stretched for hundreds of miles. Trees and bushes that grew profusely by the side of the river thinned out as the sand took control once more.

Giant cactus for a few hundred yards then scrub, then sand. Nothing but sand.

Already Dan could see that the water level had dropped by maybe three or four feet and that soon, before summer was over, the river might even dry up. Every now and then it did, leaving Black Rock Bend as the only water hole for miles.

The river started way up north in the Sierra Nevada. Rain and melted snow flooded down the mountains as the river fought its way south as it had done for hundreds of years and would, Dan hoped, for hundreds more.

The breeze was definitely cooler out here, he thought. Pity the darn rock was so hot. He breathed in deeply, noticing for the first time how clear and fresh the air tasted.

'It's beautiful out here, isn't it,' Gail said.

'It sure is. Could do with something softer to sit on though,' Dan said and Gail laughed.

She was leaning on his arm and Dan felt as if he

would catch fire. Pins and needles was setting in but he didn't want to move his arm and destroy the mood.

Gail rested her head on his shoulder and she felt him tense up.

'Are you comfortable?' she asked.

'Yes, perfectly. Thank you,' Dan replied.

'You'd be more comfortable with your arm around my shoulders,' she said.

Dan smiled at her and placed his arm round her shoulders and Gail nestled against his chest.

'Better?' she asked.

'Much,' he replied.

She lifted her face and, as Dan bent his head down, they kissed. Long, softly at first, but harder as their inhibitions left them.

They hugged and Dan, with his arms round her waist, was in seventh heaven. He'd long admired Gail, but thought he stood no chance in her affection. How wrong he'd been.

Gail, too, was having similar thoughts. Too long without a man, and this man was good and kind and gentle.

They sat, rock still, until Dan's pins and needles got too much to bear and he had to move his arm about to get the circulation going.

'Pins and needles,' he said unnecessarily.

'Oh, Dan. I'm sorry. You should have said.'

'I didn't want to lose you,' Dan said rubbing his arm and waggling his fingers.

'Better now?' she asked.

'Much.'

'Lie back,' she said, and they both lay side by side, arms around each other. Gazing up at the cloudless sky, feeling the heat of the sun and listening to distant sounds of the lapping water, was soporific and they closed their eyes, dreaming.

The shadow that was cast over them brought Dan out of his reverie first. The man was just a black silhouette, the sun directly behind him.

But he saw the gun.

'Now, ain't that a purty picture,' Pete Sidler said.

Neither Dan nor Gail could see his twisted smile.

EIGHT

Jim Warren left the Triple Bar D no wiser than when he'd arrived — except he was more suspicious now.

The ride back to town was hot and Jim could murder for a cool beer. He'd reached the last bend in the trail that led into Tumbleweed when he smelled smoke.

Looking up, he saw the white smoke billowing skywards and cursed under his breath.

Digging his heels into the horse's flanks, Jim galloped into town. The sight he saw there was one of complete chaos.

A bucket chain had been formed, but the water from the nearest trough had been all but used up and now men were running like scalded cats with half-empty buckets.

The town hall was all but lost, yellow flames and white smoke obscured most of the building. The townsfolk were more concerned with stopping the fire from spreading.

Already, timbers on adjacent buildings were smoking and the men were throwing water on the clapboards to stop them exploding into flames.

It took Jim twenty minutes to get some sort of order developed. And an hour later, Tumbleweed was at last safe from being burned to the ground.

A forlorn stone-built chimney stack was all that was left in the smouldering ruins of the town hall.

'What in the hell's bin goin' on here?' Jim bellowed as soon as soon as everything was under control.

'Hell, beats me, Jim,' Ted Wilmont said. 'One minute everythin's fine an' dandy, the next all hell breaks loose.'

'No one see anythin'?' Jim asked, although he already knew the answer to that.

'Last thing I saw was Doc Williams goin' in there,' Slim Downes piped up. 'That was 'bout an hour ago, mebbe more.'

'Jesus H.! You don't think he's still in there?' Jim said.

'If 'n he is, he ain't with us no more,' Ted Wilmont said, wiping the sweat and grime from his face.

Jim Warren glared at Ted. 'I'd better check it out,' he said and moved closer to the smoking wreck.

The heat was still far too strong for any man to get any closer.

'I'll check his surgery,' Slim volunteered.

'Thanks, Slim,' Jim said and waited until Slim returned.

'No one there, but his horse an' buggy's gone.'

'Well at least he ain't charred to a crisp,' Wilmont said.

'No one see him leave town?' Jim asked.

'Nope,' Slim said, 'but there's a note pinned to his door.'

'Why'n hell didn't you say so before?' Jim said.

'Cain't read none,' Slim said simply.

Jim looked skywards for divine intervention, none came, then stormed across to Doc Williams' place.

The note was simple and direct:

CAN BE FOUND AT BLACK ROCK BEND
D. M. Williams, MD

At least Jim knew that Dan was safe. But what was he doing in the town hall in the first place? There were no meetings arranged. What was he looking for?

Ignoring calls from both Ted and Slim, Jim walked back to his office. His head was buzzing. Frankie shot dead. Lucy Montgomery and Tom Devlin killed, and Deke Slater shot at. What the hell was going on?

He slumped down behind his desk. Fatigue filled every aching muscle and bone. What he could really do with, he thought, was a quick nap.

No chance of that, however. Try as he might, Jim could not fit all the pieces together. What reason could this Hal Warton have? Assuming, of course, that he was the guilty party?

Hadn't he already left town? He'd seen him go,

not more than seven hours ago. How far away could he be? Which direction would he be heading?

The more he thought about it, the less he knew.

The coffee pot was still on and he poured himself a cup and drank it down quickly. It was as thick as mud and tasted like it too.

Then he made up his mind.

He'd ride out to Black Rock Bend and have a word with Dan. At least he knew where he was and could ask him what he was doing in the town hall. Not that Jim suspected Dan of burning it down. He was just curious.

Wearily he left his office and walked down to his horse, which he hadn't even tethered. The animal was exactly where he'd left it, poor critter must be as tired as I am, he thought.

People were still milling around, not doing much of any good, but filled with their own importance. Kids were now trying to see who could get closest to the smouldering embers, and their mothers were yelling at them to keep away and the more they yelled the less notice they took.

Jim rode out of town slowly. People turned to watch him go, Slim called after him, but Jim just waved and rode on.

* * *

Deke Slater had a visit to make and no amount of complaining or moaning by Mrs Wiggs was going to stop him doing what he had to do.

If he was right, the whole balance of power in Tumbleweed could come crashing down – ruining the town and himself.

Deke knew he shouldn't leave his sick-bed, and a man twice his size maybe never would, but Deke was driven on by greed and guilt, and it was surprising what a man *could* do.

Mrs Wiggs had given up and, after helping him dress, she got one of the hands to saddle him a horse.

Getting on the animal was a mite harder than climbing down the stairs, but he made it, the pain in his chest began to subside as his breathing became more regular.

To the west, the sun was gradually changing colour, going from the bright yellow of the day to a fiery crimson as it began to hit the distant horizon.

Deke rode straight towards it, looking neither left nor right. In truth, every time his mount moved a stab of pain wracked his body, but he ignored it.

He had important business to attend to.

* * *

Jim Warren saw the buggy, but nothing else. What the hell was Dan doing out here? He didn't try to answer the question. He rode up to the buggy and dismounted, hitching his horse to it.

Jim wiped the inside of his hat and then, following the same path as Gail and Dan had before him, he walked up the incline.

He saw the smoke first before the smell reached

his nostrils. Then he smelled coffee.

What the hell, Dan out here making coffee!

The slug zinged off the rock by his feet. Jim was so surprised he didn't move for a second or two, hell, there was no where to hide.

Another slug ricocheted close by. Whoever was shooting at him was either a fair distance away, or he was a lousy shot.

Jim wasted no time in trying to find out which. He turned tail and ran as quickly as his riding boots would let him. Two more shots were aimed his way and again they missed.

At the foot of the incline, Jim dived for cover and got his breath back. The buggy, with his horse, and more important, his rifle, was parked about twenty feet away. Right out in the open.

Jim reasoned: If 'n he ain't hit me up on the rock, he ain't gonna hit me down here, and he crawled across the sand to get his rifle.

Another shot thudded into the sand by his left elbow and Jim gave up crawling and ran again, diving down on the blind side of the buggy.

Silence.

Breathing heavily, sweat pouring down his face both through exertion and fear, Jim reached up and slid his Winchester from its scabbard.

Now the odds were almost even, he thought. 'Cept, he knows where I am and I don't know where the hell he is.

He decided to edge his way to the east, using the rock as a barrier as best he could. He didn't know if he was moving towards the bushwhacker or away from him, but what choice did he have?

He crawled on hands and elbows, rifle gripped firmly, ready to roll if more shots rang out. But none did. Maybe he was moving in the right direction, he thought.

Unseen by Jim Warren, Pete Sidler was following his move, keeping to the rear. He'd hog-tied and gagged Dan and Gail, so wasn't worried about them giving the game away.

Hal hadn't planned this little escapade, but Pete thought Hal'd be pleased with his enterprise.

Dan turned himself over and with a great deal of effort sat up. His legs were tied at the ankles with his hands behind his back.

Gail had fainted when the bushwhacker had knocked Dan out, but she, too, was tied hand and foot.

Moving his jaw up and down, Dan tried to get the dirty rag out of his mouth, but it was tied too tight. He edged closer to Gail and saw her eyelids flutter as she regained consciousness. With his back towards her, he caressed her cheek and then motioned for her to try and sit up.

He turned his head to watch as Gail turned first on to her side, rested, then attempted to sit up. Her first effort failed, but, using Dan as a lever, she managed it the second time of asking.

Dan grunted to her, motioning to his left jacket pocket. At first Gail didn't understand what he was trying to get her to do. Then it dawned on her.

Edging backwards, she managed to get her hands into his pocket and her fingers felt the coolness of metal.

Grasping it tightly, she brought a pocket knife out into the open.

Although she couldn't make it out, Dan smiled at her from behind his gag, then, back to back, his fingers sought hers, or rather, the pocket knife.

It was hard trying to get the blade open, but eventually he managed it, then, using his fingers, he felt for the rope that secured Gail's hands together and, carefully, he began sawing.

It took him almost five minutes to cut through the rope, two more for Gail to free him. They just heard two more rifle shots and then silence.

Removing her gag, he whispered to keep quiet and pointed down the incline towards the river.

'Hide down there. Whoever he was, he crept off away from the river. I keep a rifle in the buggy, that's where I'm headed.'

'Be careful, Dan,' Gail whispered.

'I will. Now go!'

He watched as Gail slipped and slid her way down towards the river and, as soon as he was certain she was well hidden, he set off for the buggy.

Gail crouched at the foot of the granite outcrop and shook every time a shot was loosed off. In her mind's eye, she saw Dan, spreadeagled in the sand, blood forming a pool by his lifeless body. Tears sprang to her eyes, but she didn't cry. She waited – and waited.

Dan reached the buggy without hindrance and grabbed his rifle. Checking the breech, he thanked God it was loaded. The only time he ever used it was mercy killing of animals he was called out to attend to. He'd never aimed it at another human being, but he thought he might have to this day.

He cocked it, and began to make his way in the general direction of the shooting.

NINE

In great pain that was getting worse every time a hoof hit the dirt, Deke Slater made his way slowly towards the ranch of Jed Temper, the stupidly named Crow's Nest.

Deke had not seen hide nor hair of Jed in seven years, and that was seven years not long enough as far as Deke was concerned.

In their youth they were inseparable. The three of them, Deke Slater, Jed Temper and Will Harley, had grown up together, their families had been close and they'd ridden the range together, eventually finishing up in Tumbleweed in its heyday.

Back then, it appeared the town had unlimited growth potential – that was the expression Deke had used. Being on the trail heading west, wagon trains stopped over, usually at the rate of one every two weeks. They ranged in size from forty to sometimes over a hundred wagons, averaging four to a wagon. That was a lot of people and a lot of business for Tumbleweed.

Cattle drives were the next biggest earner, but

they had all too quickly dried up as the railroads began taking cattle off the hoof and shipped them back east in a quarter of the time.

That was when they'd hit upon their plan. It was to change their lives, but now, it seemed, it was about to blow up in their faces. As Deke had always said, what goes around, comes around.

The light was beginning to fail. The sun, sinking slowly in the west, would soon disappear and darkness would envelop the desert. In the distance, Deke could see the huge mast and crow's nest that Jed had transported all the way from San Francisco at a cost of nearly three hundred dollars.

Damned old fool, Deke thought to himself.

He drew rein outside Jed's home and sat there, trying to rally up enough strength to dismount. The pain in his chest had been a constant throb and he'd felt the trickle of blood ooze out from beneath his dressings and run down his stomach.

'Jed! You in there?' he shouted and the effort of shouting brought a fresh wave of pain that now began to make him feel nauseated and he literally swayed in the saddle.

'Jed!' he called again.

The front door opened a tad, and a rifle barrel was thrust through the gap. The slit of light revealed by the open door spread out towards Deke but didn't reach him.

'Who the hell's hollerin'?' a voice called back.

Deke was about to answer, he'd taken a deep breath to do so, but he was at the end of his strength. He slumped forwards, felt the pummel dig into his stomach, then slid to his left and hit the dirt.

Jed Temper heard the fall but he didn't come out. The door closed and then reopened with Jed framed in the doorway holding an oil lamp. Although not properly dark, his eyesight wasn't what it once was.

He saw the riderless horse, then he saw the crumpled body lying at the foot of his verandah. Jed now held a sideiron and the hammer was cocked. He walked forwards: 'You better git up, mister,' he said as he approached.

There was no answer. Nor could there have been. Deke Slater was dead.

*   *   *

Pete Sidler was having the time of his life. He enjoyed hunting. He enjoyed the stalk and he enjoyed the buzz that fear and adrenaline pumping through his veins gave him.

Although he'd temporarily lost sight of the rider, he knew he'd track him down and when he did, well, maybe he'd wound him some first. Maybe some leg shooting, or an an arm, maybe. Let the man know he was going to die.

The light was failing fast now, and the granite mound he was crouching on felt warmer somehow as the sun sank in the distance. Darkness could be an enemy as well as a friend, he thought.

Sidler lay rock still, straining his concentration,

trying to listen for the slightest sound, watch for the slightest movement. He heard nothing.

He stayed where he was. Hardly breathing in an effort to hear better. Still nothing.

He waited, he knew that sooner or later his quarry would give his position away.

The sun sank and instantly blackness was everywhere. Sidler blinked then closed his eyes in effort to get used to the dark more quickly.

Then he heard a sound. It came from behind him. This surprised Sidler as he'd seen the man move off to his left and ahead of him.

He altered his position. Lying flat, belly down and resting on his elbows, his rifle sat comfortably in his right shoulder, hammer cocked, finger on the trigger, with his left hand all but caressing the wooden grip under the barrel, he waited.

Silence fell on the scene once more. The moon, slow in making its presence felt, began to shine, a huge white disc in the sky, that shed an eery blue light creating black shadows that seemed to be alive. Sidler's eyes darted from one false movement to the next as cloud, too high in the sky for rain, passed across the moon's face, creating wisps of movement that didn't exist.

The temperature dropped but the rock was still warm, warmer than the air, and a fine mist had settled over the river as the heat and cold battled.

Beads of sweat formed on his cold forehead and a trickle ran down into his eyebrows where it stayed.

Jim Warren was at the base of the rock. He'd

positioned himself there so that he could use the skyline, and whatever light was left, in order to silhouette whoever it was that had been trying to bushwhack him.

What bothered him more than anything else was the whereabouts of Dan Williams. Supposing he shot Dan instead? Supposing it *was* Dan that had been shooting at him? Maybe he should call out, let Dan know who it was.

Much as he wanted to, Jim decided that calling out would be a bad move. Lying flat against the warm granite, he peered into the inky dark, looking for anything that moved or didn't look like rock.

The barrel of Sidler's rifle caught his eye. The high cloud broke and a shaft of moonlight reflected. It was all the sighting Warren needed. Levelling his own rifle, he aimed two feet behind the reflection. He only hoped it was two feet in the right direction.

Slowly, deliberately, he squeezed the trigger of his Winchester. He took up the slack of the spring and felt the trigger tense up as its resistance to the pressure he applied reached its peak. Holding his breath, Jim fired.

The rifle spat forth its deadly slug surrounded by flame. The noise of the exploding shell shattered the peace and tranquillity of the desert air and reverberated off the granite face, echoing until it seemed it would never stop.

A second shot rang out and Jim ducked. He managed to see the muzzle flash in the distance, but it pointed straight up to the sky.

Pete Sidler had never been shot before. As the bullet entered his shoulder in a straight line his finger had squeezed on the trigger of his rifle involuntarily, sending a wasted slug into the air.

The force of the hit sent Pete skidding backwards on the smooth rock. But the bullet hadn't finished its work yet. Bouncing off his shoulder blade, the slug spiralled down the inside of his chest, ripping muscle and his left lung to shreds as it went down its path of death.

Pete could feel each movement the lump of lead made right up until he could feel no more.

Jim stayed where he was. He wasn't sure whether he'd hit the man or not, or if he had whether he was dead or just wounded and waiting for Jim to make the wrong move.

From the river bed, Gail heard the two cracks as the shots exploded. Fear, already gripping the pit of her stomach, seemed to well up inside her.

'Please, God, not Dan,' she said out loud and sank to her knees.

From the other side of the rock, Dan, too, heard the shots. Instinctively he ducked down and waited. Silence. The air seemed thick and heavy and oppressive.

Dan was a doctor, not a gunfighter. He recalled in those few short moments his Hippocratic oath, and then he looked down at the rifle he was holding – the antithesis of his oath.

From ahead he heard footfalls, in the darkness he couldn't see who they belonged to.

He watched as the silhouetted figure, bent

almost double with the barrel of a rifle protruding ahead of him, made his way upwards. Dan raised his rifle, hoping against hope he wouldn't have to shoot, but knowing that, if push came to shove, he'd have to.

Sweat poured from all over his body as he waited, silently, to see what, if anything the figure would do.

The figure stooped down on one knee and Dan saw another figure, lying flat, motionless. He levelled his rifle, ready to fire if it was the wrong man dead.

Jim Warren made sure the man was dead. There was no pulse, no movement. He removed the man's rifle and sideiron before lowering his own rifle, then he removed his hat and wiped his brow with a bandanna, surprised at how cold he felt and then realized for the first time that his body was shaking almost uncontrollably.

Jim stood over the dead man looking down at his face, burning the image into his brain – it would stay there for a long time. It was the first man he'd ever killed and, he thought, it might not be the last.

Jim turned, looking back towards where he'd seen Dan's buggy parked. As he did so, the moonlight caught and reflected off his tin star. To Dan, it shone like a righteous beacon in the darkness.

'Jim?' Dan called, throwing caution to the wind.

Warren ducked down, sideiron out, aimed.

'Jim, it's me, Dan,' the voice called again.

'Dan, where the hell are you?'

'Right here,' Dan stood and clambered up the rock towards him.

'Mighty glad to see you, Dan,' Jim said reholstering his Colt.

'The feeling's quite mutual, believe me,' Dan said and the two men shook hands awkwardly.

'Gail!' Dan said suddenly.

'What?'

'I came out here with Gail when this feller bushwhacked us. Had us hog-tied down yonder. Managed to cut myself free when the shooting started.'

Both men ran down the rock carefully, each aware that it'd be plain dumb to slip in the dark and maybe break a leg.

'Gail! Gail! It's me, Dan. Can you hear me?'

'Dan, I'm here. You all right?'

'Right as rain. Jim's here with me.'

They reached Gail by the water's edge and Jim was a mite embarrassed as Dan and Gail hugged each other like they were an old married couple.

'Glad to see you're both all right,' Jim said, his back to them as he gazed across the river.

Gail released herself from Dan and gave Jim a quick hug. 'Thanks, Jim. I felt sure he was going to kill us,' she said.

'You recognize him?' Jim asked.

'Never seen him before in my life,' Dan said.

'Me neither,' Gail added.

'Well, let's get us an' the dead man back to town. I'll see if 'n I can get a handle on his identity. Give me a hand to shift him, Dan?'

'Sure.'

They loaded the body on to the back of Dan's buggy and set off back to Tumbleweed. What should have been a carefree afternoon with a woman Dan was convinced he was rapidly falling in love with, had almost turned into a nightmare.

But the nightmare wasn't over – not yet.

TEN

Molly was now hog-tied to the other chair in Will Harley's kitchen. Hal Warton ate a large meal – alone – and enjoyed every mouthful. The coffee began to whistle on the stove as he finished eating and he stood up from the table, wrapped a cloth around the handle and poured himself a mugful.

He grinned at Will and Molly as he sipped the scalding brew.

'You still ain't figured it out, have you, Will?' Hal said.

Will Harley shook his head, with the gag tied so tight, he couldn't even make a noise.

'Well, you soon will, boy. You soon will.'

Hal finished the coffee and lit up a cheroot, blowing clouds of smoke in Will's face.

'I'm goin' out fer awhiles,' he said. 'Don't you two get up to no funny business, now.' He smiled, donned his hat and locked the door behind him.

Once outside, he rigged up another booby-trap – just in case old Will *did* manage to loosen his bonds. Using a 12-gauge, he mounted it at an angle on the lean-to on the edge of the verandah, again using string to the front door handle. Any movement and both barrels would spray the entranceway with enough buckshot to kill half a dozen buffalo.

Satisfied, he mounted and set off to put the next part of his plan into operation.

*   *   *

Jed Temper loaded up the dead body of Deke Slater on to his buckboard. It took him a while to do it, Deke was no lightweight and Jed was no muscle-man. Covering the body with a blanket, Jed set off for Tumbleweed.

Although he hadn't had anything to do with Deke for a long, long time, Jed still felt a loss. It surprised him. He thought he'd be pleased to outlast both Deke and Will, but in reality he was sorry. Sorry for all the good times they'd had and sorry for all the times they'd missed.

The ride to town was uneventful. He thought of calling in at Will's place to let him know, but decided against it. He knew he wasn't too welcome there, either.

Pulling up outside Jake's place, Jed climbed down off the buckboard and hammered on the front door.

It had been weeks since Jed had been in town. He usually came in once every six or seven weeks just to provision up, maybe have a few beers, but he didn't socialize none. Kept himself to himself.

As he waited for Jake to open up, he stared

down Main Street. It was deserted. Jed knew that not many people ventured out at nights anymore, wasn't much to do anyways, but the place seemed like a ghost town.

One or two lights shone in windows, mainly behind cotton blinds. There was a light shining outside the saloon, but practically every other building was in darkness.

Jed shivered. It wasn't cold, but he shivered nonetheless. Maybe, he thought, somebody just ran across my grave.

Jake, muttering under his breath, opened the front door, oil lamp in hand; he lifted it up to see who in the hell was disturbing his peace and quiet.

'Jed? What the hell are—' Jake stopped when Jed thumbed at the buckboard.

'Deke Slater,' Jed said. 'Rode up to my house and died. Found him lyin' on the ground dead as a doorknob. Thought you might like the business.'

'Give me a hand to bring him in, Jed,' Jake said and between them they manhandled Deke into Jake's back room and laid him out on a wooden table that happened to be waiting for a body.

'Bin shot 'sfar as I can make out,' Jed said. 'Someone's even patched him up a mite.'

'Let's take a look here,' Jake unbuttoned Deke's shirt and revealed a blood soaked bandage.

'Looks like Doc Williams' work to me,' Jake said. 'Neat an' tidy bandagin'.'

'Didn't do Deke no good though, did it,' Jed said.

'Don't s'pose the doc recommended he go out a-ridin' much, either,' Jake added. 'Beer?'

'Don't mind if I do.'

* * *

Doc Williams pulled up outside the undertaker's, right behind Jed's buckboard. Gail excused herself, feeling a little the worse for wear, so Dan walked her home, promising to return, and then went back to Jake's place.

Jim studied the face of the dead man in the buggy, noting everything he could about the man. He'd already been through his pockets and found nothing, except ninety-five cents in change and four dollars' worth of folding money.

The saddle-bags had revealed nothing either. Some spare ammo, coffee, biscuits that you wouldn't feed a dog with, and a scribbled map showing the way to Tumbleweed, but not showing the point of origin.

'What d'you reckon he was heading here for?' Dan asked.

'Beats me,' Jim said. 'Unless—'

'Unless what?'

'What were you lookin' for in the town hall earlier?' Jim asked.

'How'd you know about that?'

'Never mind how. What were you doin' there?'

'Looking up the town records,' Dan said, feeling slightly uncomfortable.

'For what?'

'I don't know, exactly. I was going to look at the reports on the deaths, you know, when my parents died. And the others, of course.'

'Find anything?'

'No. I didn't get the chance. Gail – Miss Freemont – arrived and suggested we take a stroll. That's how come we were out at Black Rock Bend in the first place.' Dan paused. 'Why all the questions, Jim?'

'The town hall burned to the ground this afternoon. Took a while to get it under control, then took a while longer to make sure you weren't still in there. If 'n you hadn't left that note, we'd be a-siftin' through the ashes,' Jim said.

'Jesus! That means all the town records have gone.'

'Sure does.'

'I wanted to see if there could be some connection between the killings and Deke Slater and that stranger. What was his name?'

'Warton. Hal Warton.'

'Yes, that's right. Hal Warton.'

'Well, I guess we'll never know now,' Jim said. 'I'm goin' to the office, see if I can put a name to this here dead man. Seems I spend most o' my time as sheriff staring at Wanted posters.'

'Good luck. If you want a hand I'll come over as soon as I've seen Jake.'

'Thanks, could do with the company,' Jim said and walked off down Main.

Dan busied himself with the body, then knocked on Jake's door. It opened almost immediately.

'What now? Oh, sorry Dan. Seems like a busy night. Come on in.'

'Thanks, Jake. Got a customer for you.'

'Another one?'

'What do you mean "another one"?'

'Jed Temper's jus' brought ol' Deke in.'

'Deke Slater?'

'The same.'

'But I only saw him this afternoon. There's no way he should be dead.'

'Rode out to Jed's place and died right outside his front door,' Jake said.

'Let me take a look,' Dan said and walked past Jake to the back room.

Opening Deke's mouth Dan peered inside using the oil lamp for light. He tapped Deke's chest with his fingers and listened intently.

'Anything?' Jake asked.

'Judging by the blood in his mouth and the solid sound of his chest, my guess is he's drowned in his own blood. The ride must've opened up the wound and he's filled his lungs.'

'Jesus! What a way to go,' Jake said and spat into the spittoon set on the floor.

'I'll sign a death certificate stating that in the morning,' Dan said. 'Right now, I'm going over to see the sheriff.'

'See you, Dan,' Jake said. Jed just nodded.

Dan walked down Main and entered the sheriff's office. Once again, Jim was pouring over Wanted posters.

'Any luck?' Dan asked.

'Yup. Think so. Name was Sidler, Pete Sidler. Wanted in Texas, Kansas, Arizona, Colorado and California. Robberies, mostly, but he killed a man in Denver. Got a circular here, says that they got him in Denver. Been in the state penitentiary for ten years. Surprised he lasted that long.

'Seems they couldn't convict on the murder, got him for a bank job instead. Sounds to me like a deal was struck,' Jim said tossing the poster and circular across the table to Dan.

'So, if he's been in Tumbleweed before, it hasn't been in the last ten years,' Dan stated the obvious.

'Nope. Not unless they let him out for a ride.'

'Something doesn't pan out here, Jim.' Dan said. 'Why would he hog-tie Gail and me?'

Their conversation was disturbed by Jake rushing in, out of breath from his run.

'Sheriff, I reckon you oughtta see this!' He thrust a piece of folded paper towards Jim.

Jim took it and slowly unfolded the paper:

DAY ONE: THE SHERIFF
DAY TWO: LUCY MONTGOMERY AND DEKE SLATER
DAY THREE: WILL HARLEY
DAY FOUR: JED TEMPER
MEET ME OUT AT THE CROW'S NEST
HANK WAVERLY

'Who the hell's Hank Waverly?' Dan asked.

'Hell, I ain't heard that name in a good few years,' Jake said.

'You know him?' Jim said.

'Used to. Long time ago. Heard he got arrested in Big Bear City after what happened here,' Jake said. He looked towards Dan and lowered his eyes.

'What happened here?' Dan asked.

Jake said nothing. He looked at Jim and then back to Dan and buried his chin in his chest.

'You got something to say, Jake, you better come on out with it,' Jim said. 'I'm fumbling round in the dark, here.'

'It ain't my story, Jim. I jus' heard it from old Bill Leeson. He was the undertaker afore me.' Jake was unwilling to go on.

'Jake, I don't care whose story it is, jus' come on an' tell it!' Warren was losing his patience.

'Okay, but it's a long story.'

* * *

Molly was near to suffocating. Her gag, although not as tight as Will's, was almost covering her nostrils, and she was finding breathing difficult.

Will tried to jump his chair over to the table where a carving knife was plainly visible, but he just didn't have the strength to do it.

Molly watched as he tried and failed, and then got the message.

Summoning up strength she didn't know she had, Molly managed to jump her chair closer. The effort made her sweat and that, coupled with her breathing difficulties, slowed her down a lot.

Slowly and painfully she edged closer to the

table. The stove was pumping out heat into the kitchen and that made her sweat even more. Will Harley could only sit and watch. He was powerless to help.

With a final surge of effort, Molly moved her chair forwards, but she lost her balance. She fell, face forwards on to the wooden floorboards and, with her arms and hands to soften the blow, she went out like a light.

Will grunted as loud as he could, but Molly was hearing nothing.

Will sat and kept his eye on her. It was all he could do. For what seemed like hours he waited for Molly to regain consciousness. The pool of blood that had formed on the floor round her head had dried in the heat. Will was only thankful it hadn't grown bigger. At least, he thought, the bleeding had stopped.

Molly moved her head, tentatively at first. She was confused and still dazed by the blow on her head and for a while she hadn't a clue where she was or what she'd been trying to do.

Will breathed a sigh of relief as he saw her head move. He grunted to attract her attention. Molly turned her head towards the sound and smiled weakly at Will.

His eyes asked her if she was okay and she nodded, even though her head throbbed.

Molly was lying on her side, still bound and tied to the chair, but the chair had broken in her fall. Molly was able to work her arms free of the constricting chair back and by rocking backwards and forwards, her legs became free of the rope that tied her to the chair legs.

Carefully, with rope still wrapped round her legs and her arms behind her back, Molly raised herself on to her knees and, by resting her chin on the tabletop, she stood.

Relief flooded through her, she'd been unable to move for over two hours and now she eased the stiffness from her aching muscles.

Will grunted again and aimed his eyes at the carving knife. Molly understood.

She turned her back to the table and felt for the knife, her fingers grabbed the blade and she felt the cold steel slice into two of her fingers. She pulled her hand back, trying to see how bad the cuts were but couldn't.

More careful this time, she used her other hand to find the knife. She spun the knife round and felt with her fingertips for the wooden handle and when sure she could feel it, she slowly closed her fingers round it and breathed a sigh of relief.

Backing up to Will's chair she twisted round as far as she could to memorize the position of the rope and then, while still holding the handle, she rested the blade on the rope and began sawing.

It took Molly ten minutes to cut through the first rope. Will felt it give and he tried to help, moving his arms apart in an attempt to stretch the rope. The second strand went, and Will felt a surge of blood enter his numb fingers, the tingling sensation crept up his arm and was almost unbearable.

The third strand went and Will was able to free his hands comepletely.

It took him another ten minutes to get the use of his arms and hands back before he even attempted to free his legs, then he cut the ropes from Molly.

Molly regained her strength first and while Will rubbed his arms and legs trying to get the circulation going, she rushed to the window.

Outside was pitch black, the moon covered by cloud, she could see nothing. Grabbing hold of an oil lamp, she held it to the window. Its glow, although weak, reflected from the shotgun she saw balanced on the verandah.

Suddenly, Molly recalled the manner in which the sheriff had been killed.

'Booby-trap,' she said to Will.

'Say what?'

'He's rigged up a gun outside the door. Is there another way out?'

'Nope, one way in one way out,' Will replied.

'We'll see about that,' Molly said and, picking up the broken chair, she hurled it through the window.

Amidst the shattering of cheap glass and splintering of old wood, the noise of both barrels exploding rent the air. The thin wooden door was peppered with buckshot. Several chunks hit Will, mainly in the legs but not enough to do much damage.

Miraculously, Molly wasn't hit and in a flash she had Will's trousers down by his ankles, inspecting his wounds.

'You got tweezers?' she asked.

'Naw, never had no use for 'em,' Will replied.

'Then we better get into town, pronto. You don't want to get blood-poisoning, do you?'

The buggy was still parked outside, and as Molly pulled the door open it all but disintegrated in her hand.

'Hang on there, Molly,' Will said. 'There's a couple o' things I think I should take into town with me.'

Kneeling, Will pulled up a floorboard by the stove and retrieved a metal box. It wasn't locked. Inside were three journals, leather-bound. He removed them and put them in an empty sack and threw it over his shoulder.

'Okay. Let's go.'

Molly put her fingers to her lips silencing Will as she stood on the verandah, listening.

'You hear somethin'?' Will asked.

'No. I was just making sure. Come on, let's get out of here before he returns.'

With great difficulty, Will clambered aboard the buggy and they set off for town. First stop Doc Williams for Will, then Molly was off to find Jim Warren, the new sheriff.

She felt exhilarated at the thought of seeing Jim Warren and, in spite of her head wound which Will had assured her was nothing more than a scratch, she smiled.

Molly drove whilst Will, reloading the shotgun, sat with his sack between his legs and the shotgun, primed and ready – just in case.

The ride back to town took far less time than the ride out. The surgery was deserted. The only lights that shone came from the saloon, the undertaker's and the sheriff's office.

Molly opted for the latter.

Leaving Will on the buggy, she rushed into the sheriff's office to find Jim Warren, Jake Evans and Doc Williams, seated round the desk.

'Doc, I got a wounded Will Harley outside. We been held hostage by—'

'Don't tell me,' Jim said. 'Hal Warton!'

ELEVEN

Hal Warton studied the Crow's Nest from the safety of the night. There were no lights showing. That meant either Jed Temper was out or he was in bed. Hal couldn't see any signs of life at all, he knew there was a drive on, so maybe the place was deserted.

Parking his horse, he crept stealthily towards the small house. He stopped and listened for any sounds, but save for the breeze rustling between the house and the barns, there was silence.

Cocking his rifle, he moved forwards, sliding round the side of the house he ducked under a window, then slowly raised his head to peer inside.

Although he had his night eyes, the inside of the house was darker than it was outside and he could see nothing.

Moving towards the front of the house, he approached the front door, rifle at the ready. A board creaked under his foot and he froze. No sounds came from inside though, so he moved on.

Carefully leaning his Winchester against the

wall, he withdrew his Colt and cocked the hammer. The metallic click seemed loud enough to wake the dead, but still no movement from inside the house.

Hal Warton put his left hand on the door handle and pulled it downwards. It squeaked, metal on metal as the catch released, then he pushed the door forwards, slowly, and entered.

He stood rock still, framed in the doorway, gun ready in his right hand, his left still on the door handle. Nothing.

He walked forward in the tiny hallway and entered the kitchen. Empty. Turning, he made his way to the only other door he could see on the ground floor. It was ajar and Hal pushed it wide open before entering. Again, the room was empty.

The small staircase was set to one side of the hallway and Hal made his way there. At the foot of the stairs he stopped, his left foot on the first riser, and he listened again.

All he heard was night noises and the harder he listened the more night noises he heard.

Warton climbed the stairs.

There were three doors, all open. He entered each room in turn and was disappointed in each. The place was deserted.

He returned downstairs and hunted out an oil lamp. Lit it, and from that lit a cheroot and headed back towards the front door. As he left, he casually tossed the oil lamp back inside.

The timbers of the old house sucked greedily at the flames and the spilled oil exploded in a flash of crimson. Warton grinned, clenching the cheroot between his teeth and, without even glancing back once, he walked to his horse, mounted up and rode out into the blackness of the desert.

* * *

It took Dan five minutes to pull the pellets from Will Harley's legs. He didn't say much while he did it, and afterwards he sluiced down the small wounds with alcohol.

'Thanks, Doc. How much do I owe you?' Will asked.

'Nothing, happy to oblige.'

'That's mighty neighbourly. Anythin' I can do for you, you just say the word,' Will said.

Dan thought about that for the merest of moments. 'You ever know a man called Hank Waverly?'

Will Hartley's face grew several degrees paler at the mention of the name. Suddenly, everything became crystal clear, and he clutched his sack tight.

'Can't say I do,' he said eventually, but Dan Williams *knew* he was lying.

'Then I'll take my leave, Will. I've got work to attend to.' Dan showed Will out and returned to the sheriff's office.

'Let me check your head, Molly,' he said as he entered.

'It's okay – really.'

'Well, I'll just take a quick look and clean it up a

little,' Dan said, ignoring her.

The wound was only superficial and didn't even need a dressing.

'You'll have a nice little battle-scar,' he told her. 'Hardly noticeable.'

'Thanks.'

'Now if you'll excuse us,' Jim said.

'No, I won't excuse you at all,' Molly retorted. 'I've been held hostage and hog-tied. Anything you three want to discuss, I want to hear!'

Molly sat down, crossed her legs and folded her arms across her chest.

'Well, okay,' Jim said taking the easy option.

'Jake, you know more'n you're letting on about this Warton character. Now spill the beans.'

Jake was acutely embarrassed. He reddened slightly, then he began.

'It started off maybe six, seven years ago. Three men came into town and they each bought a small parcel of land. Things were good in them days,' Jake went on. 'Plenty o' drives coming through, wagon trains, you name it. The town was just a-bustlin' with folk.

'Well, anyways. Pretty soon, these three fellers started gettin' a mite greedy. Used to meet in the saloon every week, reg'lar as clockwork. An' when the drink got the better of 'em, well they started shootin' off their mouths about land, and wantin' more of it an' stuff.

'Well, one night this cowboy offers his services to 'em. His name was Hank Waverly an' he was a gunslinger as sure as eggs is eggs. Well they gets to talkin' an' pretty soon things start to happen round town.'

Jake paused, looking at the three expectant faces. It was Dan's face he lingered over.

'Your folks didn't die o' no disease,' he said quietly.

Dan had already begun to suspect this. 'Go on,' he said.

'Hank Waverly started "persuading" folks to sell up. Those that did, well, they got paid a fair price an' everythin', afore they moved on.

'Seems the three ranchers, that's what they liked to be called, split the land fair an' square amongst themselves.

'Then the killin' began. First off, they was made to look like accidents. A drownin' here, a trampling there. But pretty soon, there was too many "accidents", and Old Bill, well, he got a mite suspicious.

'Seems this Waverly feller had been payin' calls on every homesteader in the valley. One by one, they started to disappear. Pretty soon, all the land hereabouts, least ways, all the useful land, belonged to—'

'Deke Slater, Will Harley and Jed Temper,' Dan finished off for him.

'Yup. You got it.' Jake took a deep breath and then continued.

'Then there 'pears to have been a disagreement. Seems Waverly weren't paid his dues an' he was forced out o' town by the ranchers. Penniless, he rolled into Ghost Creek, some thirty, forty miles south o' here an' started up again. Only this time, he done got caught.

'Sheriff over to Ghost Creek came up, saying Waverly reckoned Deke, Jed an' Will, would vouch for him and maybe stand bail. But they refused, sayin' they wanted nothin' to do with him.

'Last we heard, he was tried, convicted and sent to the penitentiary. That's all I know.' Jake stopped and waited for the questions to start.

'So, for Hal Warton, read Hank Waverly,' Jim said. 'HW.'

'But why kill Tom and Lucy?' Dan asked.

' 'Cause Tom was in on it, kinda,' Jake said. 'An' Lucy, well was kinda soft on Hank at one point, but even she refused to help him outta his hole.'

'So Hank gets the help of Pete Sidler and comes here to get his revenge,' Dan said.

'That's about the size of it,' Jake agreed.

'Well, he's gonna be disappointed,' Jim said. 'Both Jed an' Will are in town. Hank'll come lookin' fer 'em an' I'll be waitin'.'

'*We'll* be waiting,' Dan said.

Jim looked up at Dan Williams. 'You ain't no gunfighter,' he said.

'No. But then again, neither are you,' Dan replied.

Jim laughed, Dan followed.

'I'm sorry, Dan,' Jake said. 'Maybe I should've told you all this when you first came back, but it didn't seem the right thing to do, at the time.'

'I presume this was all in the town records?' Dan said.

'Reckon so. Else why burn it all to hell down,' Jake said.

'Wait here,' Jim said suddenly. 'I'm gonna bring Will an' Jed over here. They got some serious questions to answer.

* * *

By the time Hal Warton got back to to the Circle C, he was madder than a scorpion on heat. A whole night had been wasted, as far as he was concerned and that dirty little sidewinder Pete hadn't showed up either.

It just about made his night when he saw the door to the Circle C house wide open – and no bodies.

He stormed into the kitchen, noticed the blood on the floor and on the table and grinned. At least they hadn't got away scot free, he thought.

He finished off the stewed coffee, checked his weapons, then, as he had with Jed's place, he burned the place out. This time, he stood and watched as the hungry flames devoured the dry wood, sending a spiral of sparks high up into the black sky.

He reasoned there was only once place they'd be now, and that was Tumbleweed. Well, Tumbleweed was going to feel the wrath of Hank Waverly – and soon.

He mounted up and, at walking pace, headed for town. He wasn't in any hurry, it was close to midnight, there wouldn't be too many people around and he knew *exactly* what he was going to do.

* * *

'You told Dan here that you never heard o' Hank Waverly. That correct, Will?' Jim asked.

Will was silent. He shifted his gaze from Jim to Jed and hung his head.

'Ain't no use a-hangin' your head,' Jim said. 'You might just as well tell me all you know.'

'What we know,' Jed interjected, 'ain't a pretty tale.'

'Pretty or not, we *need* to know,' Dan said.

The two men looked at each other and by common consent, it was Will who became spokesman.

'We was young when we rode into Tumbleweed. Good days they were too. Town all a-bustlin' an' alive. We'd been friends, me, Jed and Deke, since childhood. We always did everythin' together – share an' share alike.

'We each bought a smallholdin'. Nothing much, a few hundred acres, some cows, an' we was gonna make our fortunes. That's when the trouble started.'

Will shifted uncomfortably in his seat.

'At first things went well. Wagon trains and cattle drives, we made a good livin'. But then the wagons didn't come to town so often, and the new trail south cut the drives in half. We had to do somethin', else we'd go under.

'We started puttin' word round we wanted more land. Paid fair prices to them that wanted to sell and bit by bit, we got our land. But it was never enough.

'Then one night, over to the saloon, this feller starts a-talkin' to us. Convinces us to use him as a land-agent, or somethin'. Says that, for a price, he could get us all the land we could handle. Seemed like our prayers had been answered.'

'We didn't know *how* he was gettin' it,' Jed added.

'At first, folks came up to us, a few acres here, a few acres there an' we paid 'em off. Then this Waverly feller starts sellin' us land. A thousand acres here, a thousand acres there. An' the dyin' started.'

'We heard accidents had happened. An' we *believed* they was accidents.'

' 'Cause we wanted to,' Jed said.

'Whether we wanted to or not, we believed it. We didn't think nothin' o' the first two, maybe three. We didn't even talk about 'em. We grew richer an' richer and pretty soon we owned most o' the land hereabouts. Still do. Then Waverly started to blackmail us.

'Said he turn us all in if 'n we didn't keep him sweet. So, we paid up. Then more folks went missin'. Yours among 'em, Dan.

'We was in too deep by then. There was no way out. This feller jus' kep' killin'. We couldn't stop him,' Jed added.

'So we came up with a plan,' Will said and

stopped, his breathing deep and heavy. Sweat, already rolling down the sides of his face, seemed to double up, and he was fiddling with his fingers.

'Yeah, so what was the plan?' Jim asked.

The two men remained silent for a few minutes. The atmosphere in the small office was electric. The heat build-up made everyone feel uncomfortable. For years, Dan had *believed* what he was told. His parents dying of a fever. But he'd never checked it out. Never asked how, or why or what.

His guilt at that omission lay heavy on his shoulders. He'd been too busy building his own life. He knew he couldn't have prevented what happened to them, but when he found out they were dead, he did nothing.

'Charlie Cromer was one of the last homesteaders,' Will began. 'He had about six or seven hundred acres the other side of the river. Steers mainly, but he grew some corn an' feed. Ole Charlie was doing all right for hisself. An' he had no family.

'We set ole Charlie up,' Will said.

'Charlie had a thing about Big Bear City. Used to go there often, rented a small cabin up in the moutains. Did some fishin', huntin', got drunk a few times. Sold some o' his corn there, but that was jus' an excuse, really.

'Ole Charlie jus' loved the mountains. Well, we knew he was gettin' ready for another trip so Deke rode into Big Bear. Me an' Jed tole Waverly we wanted Charlie's place an' we told him Charlie was settin' off to Big Bear. We didn't have to say no more. Waverly took it from there.

'Deke saw the marshal at Big Bear, tole him he was worried 'bout his old friend. The marshal rode up to Charlie's cabin an', as luck would have it, caught Hank Waverly red-handed.

' 'Parently, as the marshal arrived, there was shootin' goin' on. Charlie put up a good fight, even managed to wing Waverly. But ole Charlie got hisself killed.'

'We didn't plan on that happenin',' Jed put in. 'We jus' wanted to get Waverly.'

'Anyways,' Will continued. 'The marshal saw the whole shootin' match, and Deke convinced him that Waverly had threatened ole Charlie before. It wasn't a hangin' job though. Judge at the trial sent him to prison on account that Waverly persuaded the jury he hadn't meant to kill the old man, but he had no choice.'

'We thought the matter ended there,' Jed said. 'But we should've knowed better.'

Dan stood and paced around the small room. Jim watched him as he walked.

'So Waverly killed my parents,' Dan said.

'So far as we know,' Will said. 'It was Jake who found 'em out in the desert by their wagon. They'd been there two or three days.'

'You didn't tell me you found 'em, Jake,' Dan said.

'I didn't want to tell you, that's why. It weren't no pretty sight.'

'How'd they die?' Dan demanded.

Jake fidgeted in his seat.

'Jake, I must know!'

'Couldn't swear for sure,' Jake said. 'Seems to me it must've bin poison. They was as black as coal when I found 'em. No wounds, even the vultures had left them alone.'

'Jesus!' Dan sank into a chair, he felt as if he was going to pass out.

'We didn't know, Dan,' Will said. 'I'd give anythin' to turn the clock back. But I can't. We're as guilty as Waverly. We didn't know to start with, but we *did* later on, an' we ignored it.'

The office fell oppressively silent. All the while Molly had sat and listened, shock and horror etched into her young face.

'What do we do now?' she asked.

Five pairs of eyes turned towards her, but it was Jim who spoke.

'*We* don't do anythin',' he said. 'I'm sheriff an' it's *me* that'll finish this once an' for all.'

'Not without me,' Dan said. 'I've got a vested interest in this matter.'

'You're the doc here, Dan. We might need your services. Besides, you ain't no gunman.' Jim stood. 'Will, Jed, I'm gonna lock you both up 'til I figure out what's to be done.'

Without saying a word, Will handed Jim the sack he'd been clutching since he'd left the Circle C. 'It's all in there, Jim,' he said. 'The town records. I kept 'em. I didn't want no one snooping around. I kept 'em all these years. Take 'em.'

Jim took the sack and handed it to Dan. 'You best keep hold o' this, Dan.'

Jim then led Will and Jed through to the single cell. 'Jake here'll keep guard,' he said. 'Maybe you can rustle up some extra help,' he said to Jake.

'Doubt it, but I'll try.'

'Jim,' Molly said. 'You reckon Waverly'll come back to town?'

'I reckon when he finds out you an' Will're here, it's the first thing he does. But I'll be a-waitin' on him.'

TWELVE

Although Hal Warton had calmed himself down
some after discovering both the girl and Will had
escaped, he sat and watched the house burn
down. The he set the barns ablaze and watched as
they too burned to the ground. Had anyone seen
him that dark night, seen the reflection of the
flames dance brightly in his black eyes, they
would have known the man was completely
insane.

Insane, but in control. He waited a further hour
by the blazing ruin of Will Harley's house before
deciding that Pete Sidler *wasn't* going to join him
for the final showdown.

Mentally, Warton added Sidler's name to his
death list. He lit another cheroot and mounted up.
Casting a look of satisfaction behind him at the
still blazing embers of the Circle C, he urged his
horse on.

He decided he didn't need Sidler to do what he
had to do. The Circle C was finished. The Crow's
Nest likewise. Now it was the turn of the Triple
Bar D.

Warton walked his animal, he was in no rush. The night was long and dark and no one would expect him to return. The ride took him an hour.

There was one light burning in what Warton assumed to be the bunkhouse. The rest of the ranch was both dark and as quiet as the grave. He laughed out loud as he thought that last remark. Quiet as the grave, just as well, because that's what the Triple Bar D was going to be – a grave!

He dismounted and grabbed his rifle, deciding he'd walk the last hundred yards.

The bunkhouse had to go first, he reasoned. Else the hands might be able to douse the flames. He headed towards the barn, he knew there'd be an oil lamp in there someplace, all he had to do was find it.

What he found was even better. Tucked away in the far corner, away from the stalls, was a barrel of oil – it even had a tap on it so you could get it out without spilling it.

'Thanks, Deke,' he said. 'Now watch this.'

Grabbing a bucket, Warton turned the tap on and filled it to the brim, a maniacal grin lit his face at the thought of what he was about to do.

The oil slopped on the barn floor, but it didn't bother him. The barn would go up last anyway.

He carried the bucket from the barn and approached the bunkhouse. Carefully he began pouring the oil in a huge circle round the building, splashing the walls and door as he did so. There was only one window and one door and Warton made sure there was plenty of oil in both places.

After he'd finished he stepped back, the smell of the oil filled the air and if anyone had been awake inside the bunkhouse they'd surely come running out now.

Warton fished in his vest pocket and pulled out his last cheroot. Gripping it between his teeth, he struck a match on his gunbelt and inhaled deeply. He blew out a cloud of smoke and inhaled again, all the while the match burned. Casually, he dropped the match on the trail of oil he'd left behind him and watched as it slowly made its way to the timber building.

The small yellow-blue flame danced along the ground sending a small puff of smoke into the air every now and then. It looked harmless. It was soundless until it reached the door of the bunkhouse. The explosion of bright white flame almost sucked the air from Warton's lungs. He took two or three steps backwards as the heat hit his face.

In a matter of seconds the building was surrounded by a wall of flame that licked at the dried wood façade. The glass in the window shattered as the heat built up.

Suddenly, the front door burst open and Warton saw the outlines of two men. They stood for a second or two, assessing the situation, seeing nothing but flame as the oil boiled and burned and the wood crackled its death throes.

One of the men lurched forward. He picked a bad time.

From the sloping roof, molten tar fell like wet

tears and dripped on the man. The tar burned through the man's clothes and reached his flesh and that's when he started screaming.

Warton listened to the scream dispassionately, amazed at the pitch. He didn't think a man could scream so high, sounded more like a woman to him.

As he watched, the man sank to his knees almost in supplication, a mass of flame, it was hard to distinguish his shape. Then he fell forwards on to his face and didn't move, and didn't make another sound.

The tar had formed a steady drip over the front door, and after what the second man had seen and heard, he wasn't taking any chances.

He grabbed blankets and poured drinking water over them, then he, too, attempted to escape the inferno. Warton watched as the man stood in the doorway, almost completely surrounded by flame. Any second now, Warton thought, the roof 'll cave in and that'll be the end of him.

But the man made a mad charge through the doorway, as soon as he was through the flames, he tossed the burning blankets away from him, and then checked himself for flames.

He was free, the blankets he'd tossed to the ground were burning like a funeral pyre. The man mopped his brow and stood, with his back to Warton, helplessly watching his partner burn.

Warton inhaled on his cheroot and drew his Colt. With the thumb of his right hand he cocked the hammer and loosed off a single shot.

The man who'd cheated death once, couldn't do it

a second time. The force of the impact of the slug propelled him forwards and, ironically, he landed on the still burning body of his partner. If the bullet hadn't killed him outright, then the flames that engulfed him soon did.

A crooked grin of satisfaction played on Warton's face as he watched the second man die. Then his attention went back to the bunkhouse which was now just a giant ball of flame sending sparks spiralling high into the dark night sky.

Zombie-like, Warton picked up the bucket and walked back to the barn. He refilled it, but left the tap on the oil drum open and watched as the thick oil ran freely on to the straw-covered floor.

He left the barn and walked up to the still silent house and proceeded to lay the oil around and over as much of it as he could. His attention was caught by the sound of the bunkhouse roof crashing to the ground, a giant mushroom of sparks and flame shot skywards. Warton grinned again and tossed a match into the oil surrounding the house.

Without even looking to see if it had caught, he walked straight back to the barn and set that alight as well and stood in the gap that separated the two buildings, not quite being able to make up his mind which one to watch.

If anyone could have watched him from a distance, he looked like the devil incarnate standing among the flames of hell.

* * *

It was three of the a.m. and Jim Warren was plain tuckered out. It was still less than twenty-four hours after the death of his brother, and he'd been sheriff for less than twelve. It had been the longest day of his life.

Now he was getting ready to arrest a man – at least he hoped he was – who was responsible for the deaths of over fifteen people. Jim spent twenty minutes cleaning his hand gun and his rifle, loading them and making sure they were in perfect order. He found a pair of handcuffs in the drawer of the desk, the key still in them, so he tucked them in his gunbelt.

He then decided to load a second hand gun – just in case it got to shooting time.

Jim felt remarkably calm. It surprised him. Having spent a so-far peaceful existence on a ranch, the thought of killing or being killed hadn't really sunk in. He just wanted it over.

With Will and Jed locked up in the cell, he'd sent Molly home. Dan had gone to visit Gail, making sure she was all right and Jake was in the back, armed, keeping an eye on the prisoners, as well as protecting them. How good a deterrent Jake would prove, Jim didn't know, but it was one less thing he had to worry about.

For all that this could be the last night of his life, Jim couldn't help thinking about Molly. He'd seen her around a few times, but not taken much notice. He sure noticed her now. For a moment, he closed his eyes, weariness engulfed him and he wanted nothing more than to stretch out on his bed and sleep. But he didn't. Instead he saw Molly's smiling face and, despite the situation he found himself in, he smiled.

'Want to share that smile, sheriff?'

Jim awoke from his dream with a start. He wasn't sure if he'd actually *heard* the voice or dreamed it.

He looked up to see a concerned looking Molly staring down at him, coffee pot in one hand and a plate of food in the other.

'Thought you might need this,' she said and placed both items on the desk.

Jim Warren rubbed his eyes. 'Thank you. Now you come to mention it, I am kinda hungry,' he said.

'Kinda thought you might be,' Molly smiled at him and Jim felt slightly light-headed.

Molly brought out two clean mugs from her coat pocket and placed them on the desk as well. 'Thought I'd join you in a coffee,' she said.

'I'd much rather you went home, Molly,' Jim said. 'There's no tellin' when that Warton – Waverly – feller'll come into town, an' I sure don't want you caught up in any shootin'.'

'Well thank you, kind sir, for your concern, but, as you can see, I can take care of myself.' With that, Molly pulled out a Colt hand gun from her other pocket and slammed it down on the desktop.

'That may well be,' Jim said. 'But I gotta concentrate on the job in hand and if you were around, I might just have other things on my mind.'

Molly, despite herself, blushed.

'I didn't mean to embarrass you none,' Jim said quickly.

'I'm not embarrassed, Sheriff. I'm flattered.'

'You are?'

'Yes. I am.'

Jim Warren became tongue-tied. He didn't have a clue as to what to say to that, but the expression on his face told Molly all she needed to know.

'All right, Jim,' she said and stood up, replacing the Colt in her pocket. 'I'll go home. But I want you to promise me you'll be careful. This Warton's a killer. I could tell that from the time I met him.'

'I promise,' Jim said and stood also.

'Well, enjoy your food,' Molly said.

Jim walked round the side of the desk and opened the door. 'I will.'

Without thinking, Molly tip-toed up and planted a light kiss on Jim's cheek.

'I'll be thinking of you,' she said, and walked out of the door before Jim could do or say anything, not that he could think of a single word to utter. When Molly had kissed him, he'd felt the softness of her lips and cheek and smelled that delicate perfume of womanhood and his head spun.

He was about to close the door when Dan returned.

'What the hell you doin' back here?' Jim asked.

'Well, Gail's fine and tucked up in bed by now and I figured you'd need some company. It could be a long night.'

'I already told you your services might be

needed afterwards,' Jim said.

'I know, I know. But I can sit here and keep guard while you grab some shut-eye,' Dan said. 'I've already got Slim and Ted keeping their eye on Main. If Warton rides into town, we'll know.'

Jim thought about this. There was some sense in what Dan had said.

'Okay, but you wake me up at the first sign o' trouble.'

'You can count on that, Jim.'

THIRTEEN

The night wore on. Clouds scuttered along high in the night sky alternately blocking out and then revealing the light blue disc of the moon.

Above the crackle and roar of the fires, Hal Warton could hear the distant howling of a coyote or wolf. Warton looked up at the moon and howled himself, long and loud.

The scene around Warton was a blazing inferno. No one had come out of the house, so either they'd burned to death in their sleep, or else the place was empty, Warton hoped it was the former.

He was getting bored now with the flames and although the night air had been bitingly cold, he was sweating from the heat of the flames. Time to rest up a-whiles, he thought to himself. No sense going off into town half asleep, he reasoned.

Walking slowly back to his horse, he smiled at the flames as he passed. The barn roof fell in, quickly followed by the side walls. Sparks flew high in the explosion. The house didn't flare up as quickly as the other two buildings had, but it was well alight. Come sun up, he thought, there'd be nothing left but smoking ruins.

That pleased him.

He reached his horse and pulled out the bed-roll he always carried and unrolled it on the ground. Hal Warton, alias Hank Waverly, slept the sleep of the innocent.

* * *

From his position high on the hotel roof, Ted Wilmont was sure he could see the sun coming up. An orange glow filled the night sky in the distance and he was mighty relieved to see it.

It took him some time to realize he was looking west. The orange glow he saw was fire, not sun.

Should he tell Jim Warren? He thought he should. From the position of the glow, it could only be one of two places: the Triple Bar D or the Circle C. Ted tried to get a bearing, but it was still too dark.

Leaving his rifle perched over the roof, he made his way to the back stairs. He was not an agile man and it was pitch black. In his efforts to scan the distant horizon, some of his night vision had failed him.

The flat roof beam he'd so carefully stepped over on his way up to the roof caught him by surprise as he gingerly picked his way back down.

Catching his foot on it, Ted Wilmont tripped, fell and rolled in one graceless movement. He hit the dirt with a sickening thud and he didn't move.

On the opposite side of Main, Slim Downes, the ancient barkeep, heard the thud. What little hair he had stood out on the back of his neck. What the hell was that? He decided to call out to Ted.

'Ted! Ted, you all right?'

There was, of course, no reply.

'Ted! Can you hear me?'

Nothing.

Slim Downes was not a brave man, not many men were in Tumbleweed, and the thought that the gunslinger was already back in town and picking off the lookouts one by one, didn't exactly fill him with glee.

He left his post. Maybe he'd take a look, see if Ted was okay. He wouldn't put it past the mayor to sneak off back to his bed.

As quickly as his old bones would allow, Slim climbed down the ladder to the relative safety of the ground. Once there, he crouched for a while, his ears a-bristling, trying to hear the slightest sound.

Getting his breath back – both from physical exertion and nervous energy – Slim crept round the side of the livery stable and peered across Main. He could see no movement, hear no sound. Keeping his rifle levelled, Slim stuck his head quickly round the corner of the building and looked down Main in both directions, then pulled his head back quicker than he'd stuck it out.

Nothing. Main was deserted.

Taking a deep breath, the old man charged across the street, nearly losing his footing in a wheel-rut half-way across, but he made it safely to the other side.

Panting through his wide open mouth, he again waited to get control over his breathing before moving off again. He knew Ted was atop the hotel, so turning left at bottom of the alleyway that separated the saloon from the hotel, he made his way slowly forward.

It was darker back here, what little light the moon shed, the shadows swallowed up and the inky blackness mocked him. Slim couldn't see that well in the daylight.

He found Ted Wilmont though. Or rather, his left boot found Ted.

Slim tripped over the prone body and landed flat on his face across Ted. On landing, his already primed rifle loosed off a single shot that cracked like thunder.

'Shit and shit,' Slim said, trying to pick himself up from the dirt. 'What in tarnation?'

Scrambling to sitting position, he turned to see the unconscious face of Ted Wilmont.

'So, Warton's back,' he said out loud, trying to get the jitters out of him.

*   *   *

The bullet thudded into the wall between Jed and Will as they sat silently in the single cell. For two old men, they sure fell to the ground quick enough.

It was Jake who was still sitting, leaning

against the outer wall, who was the last to hit the deck.

'Jim! Jim!' yelled Jake. 'It's a-startin'!'

Dan reached the cell first, he'd shaken Jim by the shoulder, but as he'd only just dropped off, Jim was up, gun drawn in seconds.

'Anyone hit?' Dan asked seeing the three men flat on the floor.

One by one they raised their heads. 'I don't think I'm hit,' Jake said.

'Me either,' added Will.

'Nope,' said Jed.

'Stay here, Dan, I'm goin' outside.' With that Jim left the office.

Sleep still filled his eyes, he couldn't have dozed for more than a few seconds, he thought. I ain't ready!

He listened intently and heard the chesty breathing of someone nearby. Cocking the Winchester, Jim stood at the head of the dark alleyway, trying to make sense out of the darkness.

Then he saw the figure approaching. He ducked back behind the building and waited. He heard the shuffling feet nearing and just as the man left the alleyway, Jim thrust his rifle into the man's neck.

'Hold it right there, mister,' he ordered.

Slim froze and damn near pissed his pants. 'Don't shoot, don't shoot. I'm only the barkeep!'

'Slim?'

'Jim?'

Jim Warren lowered his rifle. 'What the hell you doin' out here?'

Slim told him what he'd heard and what he'd seen.

'Ted alive?'

'I think so.'

'Right, Dan's in the office, go get him.'

Slim scuttled off.

So, Warton *was* in town. Changing direction, Jim walked passed his office and, keeping his eyes peeled on the tops as well the bottoms of the buildings, he went in search of Hal Warton.

*   *   *

The silvery fingers of dawn began to flex their muscles across the desert floor.

In the distance, Warton heard birds singing as they greeted a new day. Stiff, he raised himself up on one elbow and looked across at the charred mess that was once the Triple Bar D.

Smoke still billowed in the early morning light, but the flames had long since died out.

Standing, Warton stretched and yawned out loud. Then without further ado, he mounted up and set off for Tumbleweed.

He reined the animal in as he passed a trough that had escaped the blaze and let his horse drink its fill, then he dismounted and drank also, splashing his face afterwards with the cold water.

Warton felt good. He felt better than he had done in a long while. He was about to feel even better. He knew that Will Harley and Jed Temper were probably holed up in town, quaking in their boots, no doubt. Well, they sure had good reason to be a-quaking.

He patted his vest pockets in the forlorn hope he might have a cheroot hidden away that he maybe forgot about, but there were none left. Warton sighed. Well, he couldn't expect everything to be perfect, could he?

He decided to enjoy his walk into town, breathing in deeply through his nose and out through his mouth, he rode on as the sun rose higher and higher in the rapidly-bluing sky.

FOURTEEN

Jim Warren had searched all through town looking for Hal Warton. It wasn't until Ted Wilmont regained consciousness that the story came out.

Jim didn't know whether to laugh or cry. He'd been up all night hunting an imaginary badman – trouble was Jim knew he wouldn't stay imaginary for much longer.

Dawn arrived in Tumbleweed and the aches and pains of the previous night seemed to get put to the back of folk's minds. At least now, with daylight rapidly approaching, Jim knew his vigil would soon be over – one way or the other.

At first light, unbidden, both Gail and Molly opened up the café. They wanted to make sure the men they regarded as theirs had a hearty breakfast at least.

Ted Wilmont had a broken arm and dislocated shoulder. Dan had fixed the shoulder and set the broken bone and Ted was now propped up in bed at home with his wife fussing over him as if he was a hero – which in her eyes, he was.

Molly entered the sheriff's office breezily: 'Breakfast is ready, come and get it.'

Neither Dan nor Jim felt much like eating. Their mouths felt like the bottom of a snake pit and their stomachs were fit to bust with coffee. But they didn't argue. They knew better.

Molly took a tray to the cell and served up three meals to the inhabitants and then led Dan and Jim to the café. High on the hotel roof stood Slim, he waved as they passed, his embarrassment still evident. On the opposite side of the street, Slim had volunteered Ben Chisholm. He too gave the trio a wave as they passed.

'We'll be in the café, soon's we've done we'll relieve you. Okay?' Jim shouted to both men.

They gave him the thumbs up, then the three entered the café.

Gail put her arms around Dan and kissed him lightly on the cheek. 'Glad to see you,' she said and skitted off to the kitchen.

Jim coughed self-consciously and Molly, not to be outdone, kissed him on the cheek with a little more passion than Jim expected.

Both men sat to eat with stupid grins on their faces.

They'd only just started when they heard shouting coming from Main. They couldn't make out all the words but "sheriff" sure figured amongst them.

At the far end of Main, Jim could see the flames licking at the general store.

'Looks like he's arrived,' Jim said.

Slim and Ben left their lookout posts and scrambled to the ground as quick as their old legs would carry them.

'You two, get a bucket chain formed and see to that fire. Dan, you stay with Gail and Molly. This is my job. I got a score to settle here.'

'And you think I haven't?' Dan replied.

'No, I know you have, but there ain't no use the both of us gettin' shot up, now is there?'

'No, I guess not. But you need me you come hollerin',' Dan said and went back to the café.

*   *   *

Hal Warton watched as the two old-timers started knocking on doors and rousing the town as best they could. He also watched as Dan walked back to the café to join the two women. He remembered Gail from breakfast the day before and he certainly remembered Molly. Mentally, he added her name to his list and grinned.

Sure have some fun with that little gal, he thought. Then he set his mind to the job in hand.

Just as he had expected, his diversion had sent the sheriff to the other end of town. He'd already recced the jailhouse and seen Jed and Will eating in the cell, with another man on guard. An old man, Warton knew he'd have little trouble there.

He also knew that if Will and Jed were in jail it could only be for one of two reasons: either they'd told their story, which he didn't think they'd have the balls to do, or else they were there for their own protection – either way, they were his.

Warton checked his weapons once more. They were loaded and he was ready.

From the other end of Main, the cacophony of voices and the crackle of flame filled the still morning air. Hal Warton left the loft of the livery stable and climbed down the rickety ladder. The blacksmith was still in his cot, the thin line of blood that ran down from his bald head and nestled in his neck being the only sign left by Hal's Colt as he'd slugged him while he slept.

He left the stable and ran across Main – his most vulnerable and dangerous manoeuvre – but he got away with it. Lady Luck, he thought, is with me this fine day.

Entering the alleyway between saloon and hotel, he turned right at the bottom and made his way to the rear of the sheriff's office. The alleyway was deserted, just as he'd expected. He drew his Colt and ducked under the barred, glassless window and listened.

From inside he could hear nothing, no talk, no movement. He had to risk being seen. Straightening up, he stood to one side of the opening and slowly peered round. His Colt ready in his right hand, the first thing he saw was the opposite wall; he stood taller and looked down. The old man with the rifle was still sitting in the chair on the outside of the cell; Jed and Will, their backs to him, only a matter of two feet from the barrel of his gun, sat on the single bunk. Lady Luck wasn't smiling, Warton thought, she was positively beaming.

Slowly, deliberately, Warton aimed the short barrel at Jake: he was the only one armed, so he reasoned he had to go first. He squeezed the trigger and the slug thudded into Jake's chest. The man didn't make a sound as he slammed into the wall behind him and sank to the floor. Dead.

Will and Jed, however, *did* make a noise. Locked in the cell, they knew they had no escape, there was no way out for them.

Warton grinned malevolently. 'Remember me now, don't you boys,' he said.

'Get it over with, Waverly,' Jed said. 'We've had enough.'

'*You've* had enough. It was me stuck in that stinkin' prison! It was me out on the chain gang every day, smashing up big rocks into smaller ones! So don't go tellin' me *you've* had enough!'

'What we've had enough of is somethin' you wouldn' un'erstand,' Will said. 'We've lived with the guilt and the shame of what we were party to, an' *that's* what we can't live with, *that's* what we've had enough of. So, If 'n you're gonna shoot us, get it over with.'

Warton was seeing red, he squeezed the trigger again, the slug slammed into the far wall. Both Jed and Will had closed their eyes, thinking their time had come.

'Not that quick an' not that easy,' Warton said. 'You're gonna suffer some yet. Not as much as I had to suffer, which is a pity, but suffer you will.'

He aimed a shot at Will's thigh. The old man collapsed on the floor, pain pierced every part of his body, he lay there writhing in agony, clutching at his leg. Jed looked Warton in the eye, 'Go on, boy, do your business,' he spat with barely concealed contempt.

Warton did. He caught Jed high up in the arm and he too collapsed on the floor, neither man made a sound. Neither man would give Warton that satisfaction.

* * *

Jim had searched high and low. His initial wariness had given way to almost recklessness. The general store was ablaze, but the bucket chain had it under control, at least most of the building would be saved and Jim even had time to think that old Ted would soon be having a smoke damage sale.

Sudden realization made Jim stop in his tracks.

'Goddamnit,' he bellowed. 'Slim, take charge here, I think my business is at the other end of town!'

Jim made his way back down Main. How could he be so stupid? He should have realized what was going on here. Warton sure was a smarter cookie than Warren had given him credit for. He should have known that Warton had only one thing on his mind: revenge.

Nearing the jailhouse, Jim slowed his pace down. He peered through the dust-encrusted window, but the front office was empty, and the door to the cell was still closed.

Jim decided to check out the back. He knew there was no rear entry, but the cell had a window.

Checking his hand gun, Jim headed for the alleyway; if Warton was back there, the showdown was now!

Keeping tight to the woodwork of the buildings, Jim crept silently towards the rear of the jailhouse. He stopped, listening intently. With the noise from the far end of town, he wasn't sure whether he could hear voices or not, and decided it was better to be safe than sorry.

Crossing to the other side of the alleyway, Jim kept his back to the building and sidled down the alley, his Colt held firmly in his right hand, his left hand resting on the butt of another hand gun tucked into his belt – just in case.

He reached the bottom of the alleyway and stopped. He had no alternative now, he had to check it out and the only way of doing that was to poke his head round the corner and look.

Taking a deep breath to steady his nerves, Jim Warren took a half step forward and slowly moved his head to get a look at the back of the jailhouse.

It was deserted.

From the far end of town came a muffled explosion, Jim guessed some ammo had blown up. Should he return there and check it out? Or stay where he was?

This thing wasn't going to go away, he reasoned, nor would it until Warton was taken care of – one way or the other.

Keeping his gun levelled Jim returned down the alleyway; he intended now to check out the front of the jailhouse. It was possible that Waverly – he kept thinking of him as Warton – was playing a cat-and-mouse game with him.

Did Waverly *know* that he was here? Or was the man so intent on revenge that he'd become single-minded? Jim decided not to underestimate the man again. He assumed Waverly *knew*.

From the café, Dan Williams kept guard on Molly and Gail. His view of the jailhouse was obstructed by the livery stable that jutted out more than the café so he could only see half the building and the nearside alleyway entrance.

With no lookouts on the roof any more, a decision that Dan now regretted, there was no one who could help Jim Warren. He was on his own.

Part of Dan wanted to go out and give Jim a helping hand, but most of him was concerned with Gail and Molly. He had to protect them.

So he stood and waited, his stomach churning, his nerves as taut as steel wire.

Jim reached Main again and stopped at the corner. He was twenty feet away from the front door to his office. He moved crab-style, keeping his back to the building, closer to the entranceway.

He could see the front door stood ajar. It had been closed when he passed five minutes before.

So, Warton, or Waverly, or whatever the hell his name was, *was* inside, he reasoned. At least now, Jim thought, he had a fix.

Reaching the doorway, Jim halted and again

he breathed deeply. He seemed to be getting calmer, cooler, his brain was taking control of his body once more and he was able to concentrate more than he'd ever done in his life.

He guessed that, as this was only the second time he could ever remember his life being in danger from another human being, that he was dealing with it in the only way he knew how. Calmly and rationally.

The noise from the general store had quietened some and there wasn't the sound of crackling wood reaching him now. Something less to worry about, he thought.

Using his left boot, he slowly opened the door wider, until it would open no more. His right hand gripped the butt of the Colt more tightly, and his fingers twitched some. He drew the other hand gun and cocked the hammer.

He listened again, straining to hear any sound from within. He thought he heard grunts coming from the rear of the jailhouse, but he wasn't sure. He wanted to call out, ask if everything was okay and he almost did, but managed to stop himself.

If Waverly *knew* he was there, he didn't want to give his position away as well. Shifting forward slightly, Jim's face was now two inches away from the door-jamb. It was now or never. He sneaked a quick glance.

It was too quick for him to be able to take in all the office. So he bobbed round again. Sure the front office was clear, he was about to enter when he thought about the open door.

If Warton was smart enough to use diver-sionary tactics in the first place, maybe this was one as well. He crossed in front of the open doorway and peered through the crack between door and door jamb. No one was lurking there.

Jim Warren entered his office, both guns drawn and ready for action.

The grunts he thought he'd heard were real and they came from the cell. He put his ear to the thin wooden wall and listened. He could hear Will talking to Jed in a muffled, painful way. It was all he needed to know.

Opening the door to the cell, Jim was appalled at the sight that awaited him. He didn't have to check on Jake to see if he was dead, it was all too apparent.

The front of Jake's shirt was a crimson mess and there was a pool of drying blood soaking into the wooden floorboards. In the cell, he saw Will and Jed. They were in a great deal of pain, but alive.

'Shot through the window,' Will said, 'then he disappeared. Didn't want to kill us outright, he said. Later. Wanted us to suffer.'

'Stay calm,' Jim whispered. 'I'll get Dan over as soon as this is finished.' Jim reached across to the far wall and removed the bunch of keys hanging on a rusty nail; he unlocked the cell and opened the door, giving the keys to Will.

'Keep these safe,' he said and turned to leave.

'Good luck, Jim,' Will said.

Jim glanced at the man, then Jed and finally

Jake, but he didn't acknowledge him.

He walked into the front office and took down a Winchester from the rack, he'd left his own in the café´ with Dan. He carefully loaded it, noting his fingers had stopped shaking. Satisfied he was ready, he tentatively made his way to the front door.

It was quiet outside – too quiet by far, he thought. The sun was bright and it took him a few seconds to get used to brightness again. When he was ready, he stepped into the doorway, then on to the boardwalk.

Opposite the jailhouse, perched in his vantage point, high up in the livery stable, Hal Warton, alias Hank Waverly, saw Jim leave the jailhouse. His rifle was trained on him and he squeezed the trigger.

The slug thudded into the wall missing Jim by less than an inch. In an instant, Jim raised his rifle, crouched and let loose a volley of shots into the livery stable.

Warton was invincible. He hadn't come this far to be stopped now by some two-bit, tin-star-toting cowhand. He left the hay loft and descended the ladder to the ground. He walked, rifle at hip-height, to the large double front doors and stepped on to Main.

Jim was incredulous. Was the man mad? He didn't need no invite. Cocking the rifle, he let loose two shots in quick succession.

Warton's face didn't change expression. He refused to believe he'd been hit. Any normal man would have been flung through the air as the slugs thudded into him, but not Warton. He continued walking towards Warren, blood beginning to seep through his shirt.

He appeared in Dan's line of vision, and immediately, Dan opened the café door and raised the Winchester to his shoulder.

The Hippocratic oath was swimming round in his head as he pulled the trigger.

No a marksman in any sense of the word, Dan Williams was amazed that he'd managed to actually hit the man. He felt sick as he watched Hal Warton's head explode in a firework of blood, tissue and bone.

For what seemed like hours, the man stood rock still, then he swayed slightly, then he crumpled to the ground.

Dead.

Jim stood, amazment and relief flooded through him. He looked across at Dan and watched as he flung the rifle into the dirt.

Gail emerged from the café and threw her arms around Dan, to be followed by Molly who ran straight across Main and flung herself at Jim, tears coursing down her face in an emotional flood.

Jim Warren took her in his arms and they kissed long and hard.

They hugged and Jim whispered in her ear: 'It's over.'